'I certainly didn't ruin Derek's life!'

Andrew's voice was harsh. 'But you ruined mine.'

'What? How on earth — ?'

Bewildered, Lisa stared at him, saw that a nerve was twitching in his temple and his fists were clenched. Her eyes grew wide in astonishment while he stood silent for a few moments. Then he said grimly, 'Derek married the girl I loved. The girl I myself planned to marry.'

Dear Reader

It's a children and animals month this time, as we have NO SHADOW OF DOUBT from Abigail Gordon, and TO LOVE AGAIN by Laura MacDonald dealing with paediatrics, and VET IN A QUANDARY by Mary Bowring dealing mainly with small animals — very appropriate for spring! We also introduce new Australian author Mary Hawkins, who begins her medical career at the opposite end of the spectrum with a gentle look at the care of the elderly. Jean and Chris are delightful characters. Enjoy!

The Editor

Mary Bowring was born in Suffolk, educated in a convent school in Belgium, and joined the W.A.A.F. during World War II, when she met her husband. She began to write after the birth of her two children, and published three books about her life as a veterinary surgeon's wife before turning to Medical Romances.

Recent titles by the same author:

VETS IN OPPOSITION
VETS AT VARIANCE

VET IN A QUANDARY

BY
MARY BOWRING

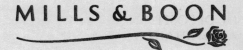

MILLS & BOON LIMITED
ETON HOUSE, 18–24 PARADISE ROAD
RICHMOND, SURREY, TW9 1SR

First published in Great Britain 1994
by Mills & Boon Limited

© Mary Bowring 1994

Australian copyright 1994
Philippine copyright 1994
This edition 1994

ISBN 0 263 78561 0

Set in 10 on 11 pt Linotron Times
03-9404-58325

Typeset in Great Britain by Centracet, Cambridge
Made and printed in Great Britain

CHAPTER ONE

LISA BENSON, M.R.C.V.S., walked into the surgery on the Monday after her holiday and found the two veterinary nurses agog with news.

Sally, the pretty redhead, welcomed her back, asked quickly if she had had a good time, then burst out, 'He's come. The new partner. He's——' she drew a long breath '—fantastically good-looking.'

Even Barbara, the steady senior nurse, lifted her brown eyes heavenwards then waited expectantly to see Lisa's reaction.

She pushed back her luxuriant copper-coloured hair with an impatient gesture, and her brilliant blue eyes were full of gentle mockery.

'What on earth have good looks got to do with it? Handsome men are often terribly conceited and think they're God's gift to women. An attitude which you seem to be doing your best to endorse.'

Sally groaned. 'I might have known it! You're only interested in him as a vet.'

'Well, that's the only thing that matters to me,' Lisa said coolly, and glanced at her watch. 'Fifteen minutes before surgery. I'll be in the office if you want me.'

She was absorbed in studying a pharmaceutical list when the door opened and a man of about thirty appeared on the threshold. For a moment Lisa stared at him, then suddenly she went very pale. As he shut the door behind him she recovered herself and held out her hand.

'You must be Mr Morland. I'm Lisa Benson.'

'Yes, I'm Andrew. Hello, Lisa.' He took her hand

and gave a puzzled smile. 'Why did you look at me in such a peculiar way? You seemed almost alarmed. Do I look so fearsome?'

She laughed. 'It was silly of me. For a moment I thought you were someone I used to know.' She paused, studying him carefully and wondering how she could have been so mistaken. He was tall and broad, with piercing hazel eyes under black eyebrows, a strong, serious face with a sensitive mouth and firm chin—well, that was different for a start. Only the dark, unruly hair and something in his features had momentarily deceived her. She said lightly, 'It was just a fleeting impression. A faint likeness to. . .' She stopped then added rather lamely, 'An old acquaintance.'

'I wonder. . .' He hesitated then added slowly, 'I have a cousin and we're supposed to look very alike. Perhaps you've met him somewhere. Derek Ashford.'

Her hand which he had retained shook in his grasp and she withdrew it quickly. His dark brows rose at the expression on her face.

'Why do you look so—so. . .?' He paused. 'You obviously know him. . . Lisa Benson—why, of course. . .' He stared at her, his eyes blazing. 'You're the girl who ditched him at the last moment. A week before the wedding.' He stood back, his mouth set in a grim line. 'Good God! If I'd known you were here. . .'

Speechless for a few moments, her heart pounding so fast that she felt almost faint, Lisa drew a long breath in an effort to pull herself together. Then as anger took over she found her voice.

'So I changed my mind. I realised I'd made a mistake. It was better to break things off rather than commit myself and Derek to a marriage that could only have ended in tears.'

His eyes filled with scorn. 'Why don't you tell the

truth? You'd found someone else, hadn't you? Someone you'd been playing with behind your fiancé's back.'

Her face flamed. She stared up at him as he towered over her, almost threatening in his fury—fury that seemed quite inexplicable and out of all proportion. Then as his last words sank in she said coldly, 'How dare you say that when you know nothing about it? Richard Walton was an old friend—we were at college together. He stood by me when I needed advice. He understood my problem, which is more than you do.' She paused for a moment, then added sharply, 'In any case, what on earth has it got to do with you? If Derek had been your brother it might seem a bit more reasonable, but to get so worked up because of something that happened to a cousin is ridiculous.'

His mouth twisted cynically. 'You may have been able to fool Richard Walton, but you can't fool me. I'm glad I've found you out so soon. Otherwise——' he stood back and surveyed her in an all-enveloping gaze '—to a normal sensual male like me you would be temptation itself. In spite of the fact that you are so beautiful—your fantastic blue eyes alone are a man trap, and your wonderful hair and figure—in spite of all that, you are hard, selfish and callous. Only one thing puzzles me, and that is that you're a vet. A caring profession—it seems completely out of character.'

Lisa gasped. 'How can you say such a dreadful thing?' She swallowed hard, near to tears. Then, determined that he shouldn't see how his contemptuous words had wounded her, she said mockingly, 'All because I'm supposed to have let your cousin down. What a mountain to make out of a molehill.' Then, as she saw him about to retort, she added quickly, 'And you surely know that Derek married someone else soon afterwards. He didn't suffer for long, did he? I certainly didn't ruin his life.'

His voice was harsh. 'But you ruined mine.'

'What? How on earth. . .?'

Bewildered, she stared at him, saw that a nerve was twitching in his temple and his fists were clenched. Her eyes grew wide in astonishment while he stood silent for a few moments. Then he said grimly, 'Derek married the girl I loved, the girl I myself had planned to marry.'

She drew a long breath. So that was the reason for his unaccountable anger. But was she supposed to take the blame for his disappointment? She said coldly, 'If the girl you loved preferred your cousin it was just as well you didn't marry her. I probably did you a good turn.'

'Of all the heartless. . .' His eyes blazed down at her again so fiercely that she drew back a step. Then, taking a grip on himself, he said icily, 'You'd better keep out of my way as much as possible. In fact it might be advisable if you started looking out for a job in another practice.'

She turned scarlet, staring at him incredulously. 'Are you sacking me? You've no right.'

'Oh, yes, I have. I'm the new partner, remember. But I'm not actually sacking you. I'm just giving you warning that if you stay here I shall make your life so unpleasant that you will be glad to leave.' Turning on his heel, he went out, leaving her staring after him, her mind in turmoil.

It was as though a hurricane had roared through her life, destroying everything she had built up. The eventual partnership in this practice that James, her employer, had promised her, that was now out of the question, and her hitherto contented existence would be darkened by this newcomer who had so horribly misjudged her. Remembering her real reason for abandoning her marriage plans, she felt her bitterness increase. She could, if she wished, destroy in a few words the illusion he obviously still cherished about his former love. In fact, she owed it to herself to enlighten him and would have done so if he had only given her the chance. Still tense with anger, she decided to keep her secret to herself for the present. One day, a day of her own choosing, she would tell him the whole story and humiliate him as he had just humiliated her. Bracing herself, she had just managed to get calm when the door opened again.

'There are clients in the waiting-room.' His voice was hard. 'Surgery should have started ten minutes ago.'

'Well, you're to blame for that,' she said scornfully and swept past him, her head held high.

Somehow she got through the next hour, working her way through a variety of cases, examining each patient with care, listening to their worried owners, and finally using her diagnostic skill to determine the cause of each problem. Then, before starting on the operations fixed for that morning, she made an excuse and escaped up to her flat over the surgery, leaving Barbara and Sally to have their coffee break alone.

Gazing out of the window, she saw James Carter walking down the yard with his new partner. James looked rather frail, but that was not surprising after the alarming heart attack he had recently experienced, and the contrast between him and the much younger man was very noticeable. But that handsome exterior was just a shell that covered up the ruthless, revengeful man who had attacked her so fiercely without allowing her a moment in which to defend herself. She watched them anxiously as they strolled along. Was she the subject of their conversation? Was Andrew Morland already telling James that he wished to get rid of her? Of one thing she was certain: unless he revealed the real reason for his animosity towards her he would never persuade

James. Why, just before she had gone on holiday James had praised her work, congratulated himself on having at last found the right person to run the small-animal side of the practice, and promised her an eventual partnership. Frowningly she watched the two men until they disappeared into the kennels at the end of the yard, then, turning away from the window, she comforted herself with the sudden conviction that they were only doing a tour of inspection. She glanced at her watch. No more time in which to reflect on her personal problems. There were two cats and a dog awaiting operations. As she made her way downstairs she resolved that work and worry must be kept strictly apart. There was no way in which she would allow Andrew Morland's hostility knock her off balance.

Barbara and Sally looked at her with open interest when she joined them, and Barbara said, 'We couldn't help hearing your raised voices when you and Andrew were in the office. What on earth was it all about?'

Before Lisa could think of a reply Sally said, 'Unfortunately we couldn't listen because there was a bit of a ding-dong between two dogs in the waiting-room, so come on — do tell.'

Lisa managed a laugh. Their curiosity was so friendly that it was impossible to take offence. It was equally impossible to enlighten them, so, thinking quickly, she said lightly, 'Well, it was all rather silly. A misunderstanding. I thought he was someone else — someone I knew in the past. He looked very like him. This man he resembled — well, he had made me very unhappy and Andrew happened to have heard all about it. We disagreed on the rights and wrongs of the affair. That's all.'

They gazed at her in silence, plainly wanting to know more, but she turned briskly away and went towards the cat baskets standing against the wall.

'We'll do these first,' she said firmly and, with a quick glance at each other, the two nurses began the necessary preparations.

Working silently and skilfully, Lisa was thankful that she was able to concentrate on her patients to the exclusion of all else. As soon as the cats were placed in warm recovery cages she began on the Labrador. A tumour was removed, then as she finished suturing the wound Barbara said, 'Mr Barrett is coming in for a consultation about his old dog. He rang up when you were upstairs. He should be here soon.' She paused. 'The dog is fifteen years old.'

Lisa sighed. 'That looks like being a sad story. Well, I shan't want you both here.'

'I'll go and clean the kennels,' Sally said quickly. 'I simply hate seeing animals put to sleep, and that's what it sounds like. I'm not as hardened to it as Barbara.'

'I'm not hard,' Barbara said indignantly. 'I hate it too. But it's not the animals that upset me — it's a merciful end for most of them. It's the owners I'm sorry for.'

Lisa nodded thoughtfully. 'You're right. It's terribly sad to have to break up a loving relationship, especially when sometimes it's all an old person has in life. It's one of the most emotional sides of veterinary work.'

Mr Barrett came in a few minutes later, a man in his sixties with a worn, anxious face and tired eyes that filled with tears as he watched Lisa examine his beloved dog. The little black mongrel submitted listlessly to her gentle hands, and her heart sank when the time came to give her verdict.

'It's old age, I'm afraid, and we haven't any cure for that. His heart is in a bad state, he's nearly blind and. . .' She stopped and stroked the shaggy head compassionately. 'Poor old boy. I'm afraid he's come to the end of the road.'

There was silence for a few moments, then Mr Barrett said quietly, 'I don't want him to suffer. Will you do the necessary, please? Do you mind if I stay with him to the last?'

'It's the kindest thing you can do.' Lisa's eyes were misty as she watched him put his arm round his old friend and whisper softly to him. The dog's tail waved slowly and, lifting his head, he licked his master's chin lovingly. At last Mr Barrett looked up.

'You can put that needle in now, miss,' he said.

It was all over very quickly, and a short time later he gathered the little body up into his arms.

'I'll bury him in the garden,' he said, and Lisa nodded understandingly as she said goodbye.

Barbara had just poured out much-needed coffee when they were interrupted by an agitated woman carrying a Jack Russell terrier.

'Jackie has just snapped at a wasp. He's been stung on the tongue and he's in trouble. His tongue is swelling up — he's beginning to choke.'

Placing the unhappy little dog on the surgery table, she stood back, wringing her hands, and looked at Lisa appealingly.

An injection of antihistamine quickly administered soon solved the problem, and a few minutes later Lisa said, 'It's all right. We've got it in time. I'd like to watch him for a little while, so have a coffee with us.'

Announcing herself as Mrs Webster, their client asked, 'What can you do with a dog who snaps at flies, moths, bees and now a wasp? Anything on the wing, in fact. The wasp season isn't over yet, so how can I prevent this happening again?'

Lisa smiled. 'I think you'll find he's learnt his lesson. He'll probably run for cover now when anything buzzes near him. You can help by using a warning tone — show him you're frightened too. He may eventually even get a bit neurotic about flying insects, but that's surely better than snapping at them.'

'Well, that's that,' Barbara said thankfully as Mrs Webster went out, but a minute later Sally, coming back from the kennels, announced,

'There's a boy in the waiting-room. Shall I tell him surgery is over?'

'Goodness, no,' Lisa said, 'we can't stick rigidly to the clock. Let him in, please.'

The client was a boy of about sixteen, who grinned as he placed a cardboard carton on the table.

'Reggie's got a spot of ear trouble,' he said and took out a large brown rat, causing Sally to give a little shriek of disgust and draw back hastily. 'You shouldn't frighten him like that,' said his owner reproachfully. 'He's very sensitive to noise.'

Holding his pet firmly, he said, 'It's all right, Reggie, no need to try and run away. I'm here.' But the rodent scratched frantically at the table with feet that looked like little hands. Its tapering tail was almost as long as its body, its eyes looked like black shoe buttons, and its whiskers twitched rapidly on its pointed nose.

Holding him firmly, the boy said proudly, 'He was best rat in the show a month ago. He's a real champion. Look at his fur — perfect texture — and his tail — not a bit scaly.'

Sally shuddered and Lisa laughed.

'Mind you don't let him go or you'll have my nurse here in hysterics. She's new to this work.' She paused. 'Pass me my auriscope, please, Barbara.'

A few minutes later, having thoroughly examined both ears, she looked up. 'The usual thing — mites. He's probably picked them up at the show. They take two or three weeks to develop.' Reaching out, she took down a bottle from a shelf. 'These are anti-mite drops. I'll put in a couple now and then you must continue the treatment—a drop a day in each ear for four or five days. After that, I advise you to treat the ears once a month to keep them clear.'

Whiskers still twitching, Reggie was picked up by his young master and deposited once more in the cardboard carton. As he went away the boy cast a reproachful look at Sally.

'Can't think why you don't like rats. They make awfully good pets.'

Sally waited until the door closed behind him, then, heaving a sigh of relief, she said feelingly, 'Good pets or not, I never want to see another one.'

Lisa laughed as she washed her hands. 'I don't like them much either, but I look at it like this: all animals have their part to play in Nature, and although some are repellent they're all interesting.'

Sally shook her head. 'I think the world would get along very nicely without them and the sooner they're extinct the better.'

Barbara said thoughtfully, 'I believe the rat is one of the few wild animals that is actually increasing in number.'

'Good grief!' Sally stared. 'That's enough to give me nightmares.' She paused. 'Still, I suppose there are worse things. Snakes, for instance. Now the moment one of those is brought in you won't see me for miles.'

Lisa shrugged. 'It all makes for variety. A change from all the dogs and cats, though of course they form the majority of our patients.' She turned to Barbara. 'It's your turn for a few hours off duty. Sally will hold the fort while I get on with some paperwork.'

When the telephone rang she paid no attention, knowing that Sally would deal with it if it were a routine call. But a minute later the door opened and Sally said,

'I thought I'd better tell you, but I don't think it's urgent. Mr Rowton from Lea Farm says a cow calved yesterday but now her calf bed is out. I didn't like to tell him that I hadn't the faintest idea what he was talking about.'

Lisa got up quickly. 'It's urgent all right. It means the cow's uterus is out. "Calf-bed" — uterus. See?'

Sally giggled. 'These farmers speak another language. "Wooden-tongue" — "blown cow". . .'

'I could tell you a few more, but there isn't time now. Get through to Andrew on his car phone, will you?' She paused. 'No, listen — someone in the waiting-room; I can hear a cat miaowing. You'd better look in there. I'll ring Andrew.'

She announced herself, gave the message, and added, 'Would you like me to give you directions for finding Lea Farm? It's rather hidden away.'

'I know where it is, thank you. I'm not a stranger to this area. I grew up not far from here.'

Lisa put down the receiver and stood gazing down at it, looking puzzled. She herself came from the north of England, as did Derek and Jane. So how could Andrew ever have got involved with Jane, who, as Lisa knew, had never moved away from her home town? Then suddenly she remembered that Derek was Andrew's cousin and, at some time or other, Andrew, while on a visit, must have encountered Jane. Her puzzled thoughts were interrupted as a small girl carrying a cardboard carton was ushered in by Sally.

The child looked up at Lisa fearfully. 'This cat, 'e keeps coming round to our house and me mum don't like animals. She says you'll know what to do wiv 'im.' Placing the carton on the table, she added tremulously, ''E's a lovely cat. You won't put 'im to sleep, will you?'

He was indeed a lovely cat, a fully grown coal-black tom with one white spot on his chest. He stared back at Lisa with brilliant green eyes and began to purr loudly as she stroked him gently.

'Goodness knows why he's purring,' she said. 'He's very thin. Poor thing. I should think he's been lost for some time.'

'I gave him some milk,' the little girl said defensively, 'but me mum said I wasn't to give 'im no more or he'd think he belonged to us. She said the only way to get rid of him was to take 'im to the vet.' There was silence for a moment and tears began to run down the child's face. 'Whatcher going to do with 'im, miss?'

'Well, I'm not going to put him to sleep, that's for sure,' said Lisa consolingly. 'I'll find him a good home and, what's more, I'll give him a meal right now. You can watch if you like.'

A bowl of cat food was quickly demolished, and the child went away, comforted by Lisa's promise. Sally laughed as she placed the purring tom in a cage.

'No question of payment, of course. People seem to think that vets live on thin air.' She paused. 'Shall I look up the list of missing animals?'

Lisa nodded. 'Let's hope he answers to someone's description of their lost pet, otherwise I'm landed with the usual problem. If I kept every stray that was brought in there'd be no room in my flat for me. And as for payment — well, it certainly wasn't up to that child's mother; she was actually doing the kindest thing she could think of.'

They had almost given up hope when at last they found the description they wanted.

"Answers to the name of Spot'.' Lisa laughed. 'Well, I suppose we ought to have guessed that. Let's ring the number and give the good news.'

The delighted owner lived quite near the surgery and said she'd be round in ten minutes. When she arrived Sally gazed at her in open admiration. She was about thirty-four, and very smart, slim and tall, with silvery blonde hair cut in a sleek short style. She stood cuddling

Spot and laughed as his purrs almost drowned her voice.

'I'm Olivia Claydon and I only moved down here three weeks ago. Spot went missing the next day. I'd almost given him up.' She paused. 'I'm quite new to this part of Sussex and I haven't met many people yet. My brother is a doctor who has just taken up a new post in the local health centre and, as his wife is dead and I'm divorced, I live with him and help part-time in the reception office of the centre. I've been very upset at losing Spot and asked everyone if they'd seen him. I've even waylaid your Mr Morland—he lives in that lovely house standing alone down the lane just off the road where my brother and I live.' She stopped, hesitated for a moment, then added, 'He's a real charmer, isn't he? I've seen a woman who seems to run the house, but she obviously isn't his wife. Is he married?'

Sally giggled, then quickly turned it into a cough, and Lisa suppressed a smile. 'No,' she said, 'he's not married. He's our new partner.'

'Hmm.' Olivia looked pleased and her green eyes glinted a little, but she said no more. When she had gone Sally burst out laughing.

'Goodness! She's obviously on the look-out for another man. I should think Andrew will be an easy prey. I'd better warn Barbara that our chances begin to look slim.'

'You're incorrigible, Sally——' Lisa laughed in spite of herself '—but I shouldn't think a woman with her looks and expensive clothes would want to ensnare a very ordinary vet.'

'Oh, but he's not ordinary. Didn't you know? He inherited lots of money when his parents died. They were killed in an air crash. His father was one of James's oldest friends—that's why Andrew accepted his offer of a partnership. He's. . .' She stopped and giggled at the astonished look on Lisa's face.

'For heaven's sake! How do you know all this? He's only been here a fortnight.'

Sally shrugged. 'Mrs Scamell told me when she bought her dog in for a booster injection. She works for him—cleans the house and cooks.' She stopped as she saw the frown on Lisa's face and added defensively, 'I didn't ask her. Andrew gave the injection—it was when you were away—then he had to rush off to an appointment and she hung around for a while and talked, poured it all out—rather like Olivia Claydon did just now.'

'Well, I expect it's all very exaggerated. If it's true, why does he work here? I would have thought he'd be leading a very different kind of life, like most rich people do.' Lisa's tone was scornful, and Sally looked surprised.

'Why shouldn't he work? Anyway, Mrs Scamell says he told her he likes animals better than people.'

'You're as bad a gossip as Mrs Scamell,' Lisa said reproachfully, 'but I think you ought to be a bit more careful. I hope there was nobody else in the room when Mrs Scamell was talking about her employer.'

'Of course not,' Sally said indignantly. 'I know better than that, but I couldn't help listening to her. As for why he isn't swanning around with all the beautiful people, I haven't a clue. You'd better ask him yourself.'

'That's likely!' Lisa laughed. 'In any case, I'm not interested in his private life. I just hope that, as James's partner, he won't start changing things around here too much.'

Back in the office, she found it difficult to concentrate on her work. It was evident that Andrew was, in reality, going to change everything. Now, instead of easygoing James, she would have to defer to a man who disliked her as much as she disliked him. Would he really make things so unpleasant for her that she would be forced to resign? He would undoubtedly try, but she must fight him all the way. She could, she knew, put an end to his antagonism by telling him the truth about his lost love, but as he had refused to listen to her he must wait to be enlightened. He had humiliated her, but in the end she would make him eat humble pie.

It was during evening surgery that another problem arose. There were so many clients in the waiting-room that it was obvious the surgery hour would have to be extended in order to deal with them. And a few difficult patients with owners unable to control them made matters worse. Lisa sighed to herself as she saw Sally constantly glancing at her watch, but it was Barbara who spoke sharply to her.

'It's no use, Sally. This isn't the kind of job where the office closes at the same time every day. You'll have to get used to being late.'

Seeing the resentful look on the younger girl's face, Lisa asked, 'Have you got a date?'

'Yes. I'm supposed to be meeting Dave at seven-thirty, and he gets terribly mad if he's kept waiting.'

Barbara frowned and began to say something, but Lisa shrugged and said quietly, 'All right. Just this once. Off you go, but try to make Dave understand that you can't always get away on time.'

She was gone in a flash, and Lisa looked ruefully at her senior nurse.

'She's very young and she's not really as essential to me as you are.'

'I sometimes wonder if she'll make the grade,' said Barbara. 'She's beginning to realise that veterinary work isn't as romantic as she imagined, and this demanding boyfriend doesn't help. From what she's said to me he sounds a dreadful type, but he's very good-looking and Sally's besotted by him.'

'Oh, dear.' Lisa sighed. 'I can see trouble ahead. What's more, with surgeries like this most evenings, we're going to need more staff.'

'Do you mean another assistant or another nurse?' Barbara asked, and Lisa shrugged.

'Both, I rather think. Still, that's not for me to decide. Let's have the next patient in.'

A shaggy dog of uncertain breed, friendly and full of life, was apparently giving his owner a difficult time.

'I'm Miss Stevens and this is Harry. He's a problem.' She frowned as Harry tugged at his lead in an endeavour to explore the room. 'He's driving me mad. He chews up carpets and tears at doors and it's almost impossible to house-train him. Someone suggested a course of tranquillisers might be the answer, so that's why I've come to you.'

Lisa frowned. 'That's a bit drastic, isn't it?' She gazed down at the so-called problem, who stood panting and waving a large feathery tail, his expressive eyes full of life and suppressed energy. 'Come on, boy. Let's have a look at you.'

With Barbara's much needed help he was placed on the table and thoroughly examined. Then Lisa said, 'He's physically absolutely fit. No reason for his difficult behaviour unless. . .' She paused, knowing that she must be tactful with this obviously very tense owner. A little detective work with regard to Harry's home life would, she felt sure, supply the answer to Miss Stevens' predicament. After a few careful question and rather sulky answers she gave her verdict.

'It's my considered opinion that Harry does all this damage through sheer boredom. You say you have to leave him alone for most of the day. You also say that the school where you teach is quite near your home.

Could you not give up some of your lunch-hour and take him for a short walk? Also, before you leave in the morning a quick run would be better than just turning him out in a small garden. Then, of course, when you get home at the end of the day he should have a proper walk — a dog this size requires quite a bit of exercise. I feel pretty sure that would put an end to his rebellion at what must be, to him, a frustrated existence.'

'Oh, my goodness!' Miss Stevens stared at Lisa incredulously. 'I'll never have time for all that. I bought Harry to be a guard dog. Living alone one gets nervous.'

'Perhaps a neighbour could help out? A friend? Some retired man with time on his hands?'

Miss Stevens shrugged irritably. 'I'll have to think about that, but, as I said, I really want some pills to keep him quiet in the house.'

'If you dope him up he won't be much use as a guard dog.' Lisa looked at her obstinate client appealingly. 'Do try out what I've suggested. A dog needs regular exercise — it's cruel to deprive him of that.'

Obviously dissatisfied, Miss Stevens departed, and Lisa sighed. 'People like that shouldn't keep dogs. Left alone all day — it's not surprising they tear the place to bits. I would if I were a dog.' She sighed again. 'Well, let's have the next patient.'

She was examining a cat when the outer door opened and, looking up, she found Andrew facing her. He said coldly, 'You've got at least a dozen more patients out there. Do they always come in as late at this? Can't you organise things so that they come in at the proper time instead of turning up when the surgery hour is nearly over?'

Resentful at the criticism, Lisa said sharply, 'The

waiting-room was already full at the beginning — people just keep coming.'

'Do you have many evening surgeries like this?'

'Quite often. The small animal side of this practice is increasing. Lots of new housing estates — consequently more pets.'

Her face flushed, she turned back to her patient on the table and saw that the owner had been listening with open interest. When the necessary injection had been given, along with instructions on treatment at home, Barbara led patient and owner out and Lisa turned to Andrew.

'I think you might have waited till my client had gone before rebuking me like that. Or is this part of your plan to make life unpleasant for me?'

To her surprise he apologised quickly. 'Of course not. I spoke in the heat of the moment. I'm sorry.' He paused, gazing at her thoughtfully. 'As for the plan, as you call it, I've changed my mind. James apparently thinks very highly of you and is contemplating offering you a partnership in the near future, and I can see that you merit it. So I take back what I said about forcing you to leave.'

Astonished and incredulous, Lisa found it impossible to believe. Surely, she thought confusedly, there must be some trickery behind his conciliatory tone. She said coldly, 'First of all you bully and try to blackmail me and now you're all sweetness and light. I would be a fool to believe anything you say.'

His eyes glinted and the colour left his face. He opened his mouth to retort furiously, but at that moment Barbara came into the room, leading with difficulty a large German Shepherd dog. She laughed ruefully. 'Hugo only needs his nails cutting, but Mrs Grant can't control him and prefers to stay in the waiting-room. She says she doesn't want to see the

struggle.' Pulling the reluctant dog towards the table,
she added, 'Thank goodness you're still here, Andrew.'

He smiled grimly, took the lead, and shortened it in
his grasp. As soon as the table was lowered he hoisted
Hugo on to it. Held in an iron grip, the dog capitulated,
and Lisa was able to trim the nails on each foot without
difficulty. As Barbara led him triumphantly back to his
mistress Lisa said coolly, 'Well, thank you very much.
I've no doubt we should have coped somehow, but you
certainly made it easier for us.'

He smiled cynically and shrugged. Then he said,
'Obviously these busy surgeries are a credit to your
work here. Things were pretty quiet while you were on
holiday. I gathered the locum wasn't very popular with
the clients. But you can't go on without some extra
help. Struggling with a great dog like that at the end of
a hard day is no joke. I think we'd better get another
assistant in — one who can share the surgeries. I'll speak
to James about it. Meantime ——' he jerked his head
towards the waiting-room ' — I'll do the rest tonight.'

For a moment Lisa was nonplussed. This decision
was too peremptory for her liking. Ungratefully she
said, 'I have a patient coming in soon — a possible
pyometra. It has to be discussed with the owners — I
can't just disappear.'

He shrugged. 'Very well, but I suggest you make
yourself some tea and take it in the office. I'll call you
when necessary.'

With no desire for tea, Lisa sat down at the office
desk and reflected on Andrew's high-handed treatment.
But she had to admit that she was glad to have a rest.
Her mind revolved around the idea of another assistant,
and she began to work out the pros and cons. It would
certainly help with the workload, but there were days
when the surgeries went suddenly quiet, and then the
extra assistant would be superfluous. Perhaps an assistant

to come in part-time. A vet who was semi-retired or an overseas graduate in search of experience. Surely someone like that would fill the bill? She had just resolved to put this idea forward when Andrew called to her to see her problem patient.

The examination of the Labrador bitch completed, she looked up at the anxious owner.

'Those tablets worked for a while, but now —— ' she shook her head ' — it can't be left any longer. She's not too old. I'm pretty sure she'll stand the operation, and it will give her a new lease of life.'

She fixed the time, gave the necessary instructions, and accompanied her client to the door. She was about to go into the office to thank Andrew for his help when he emerged. Before she could speak, the surgery door opened and a young boy came in, carrying a kind of cage. He looked up at Andrew.

'Do you know anything about grass snakes?'

'Well, yes, I do but —— ' Andrew indicated Lisa ' — I expect this lady is the veterinary surgeon you want to see.'

'Oh. . .' The boy turned to survey Lisa, who gazed back at him with a quizzical smile.. 'I shouldn't have thought. . .' He shrugged. 'Well, anyhow, I found this grass snake about a month ago and decided to keep it as a pet. The trouble is, it won't eat anything and its getting thinner and thinner.'

'Oh, dear. Well, open the cage and let's have a look at him.'

The patient was olive-green with several rows of black spots running the entire length of its back. There was also a pale yellow mark, like a collar, on each side of the neck. Placed on the table, it lay as though dead.

Lisa said, 'It certainly is very thin. What have you offered it for food?'

The boy hesitated. 'Well, my friend tells me it's got

to have live food — things like frogs and newts — but. . . well, I just can't. . .'

Lisa nodded sympathetically. 'I know how you feel. I couldn't either.' She paused. 'That's a very good reason for not keeping it as a pet. I realise it doesn't need feeding very often — about once a fortnight or more — but it must have water and should be kept in damp conditions.'

'I've tried dangling bits of raw meat on a string to make him think it's something live, but —— ' the boy shrugged and shook his head 'I can't fool him. I've had him three weeks. Is he going to die?'

'He will if you don't soon take him back to the stream or marsh where you found him.' Lisa paused then added, 'Why not do that? It's not kind to keep a creature like this, you know. At least I don't think so.' She turned to Andrew, who had stayed silent. 'What do you think?'

He nodded. 'I agree with you entirely.' He turned to the boy. 'I tried to keep one when I was about your age, but I had to release it eventually as I couldn't bring myself to give it live things like frogs.' He paused. 'It has to feed that way because its tiny sharp teeth can only be used for gripping its prey. Poor creatures — they're completely defenceless.' He stopped for a moment, then, seeing the disappointment on the boy's face, he added, 'Why not keep lizards? They're very rewarding. I had a lizardry in my garden when I was about your age. It's easy to build, and the lizards thrive. It was nice to see them come out of hibernation on the first warm days of spring and bask in the sunshine. They laid eggs and hatched them out. They kill small insects before swallowing them.' He looked down at the unfortunate grass snake. 'The sooner this poor fellow is returned to his natural habitat, the better.'

The boy nodded solemnly and, picking up his pet, he

returned it to its temporary home. 'I'll put it back today and I'll go in for lizards.' He fumbled in his jacket pocket. 'How much, miss?'

'Nothing at all.' Lisa laughed. 'I'm glad you're going to do the right thing.'

When the door closed Lisa went into the office, followed closely by Andrew.

'About your idea for an additional assistant. . .' she said, and proceeded to put forward her suggestion.

The atmosphere between them seemed to have settled into a calm professional one, and he listened carefully to her proposition. But when he spoke it was apparent that his enmity was still there under the veneer of businesslike talk. He said slowly, 'It might work. After all, you might decide to leave the practice, and if that happened we would probably have to find someone at short notice.'

Lisa caught her breath. So that was how his mind was working. It would be a good way of easing her out and of causing the least inconvenience to the practice. She flushed angrily. 'I might have known you'd see it like that. I was thinking of the practice, but you're thinking only of easing me out.'

He gazed at her frowningly. 'You misunderstand me. I have no ulterior motive. But unless you take up an eventual partnership here you will most probably move on of your own accord. It would be the natural thing to do. Or you might get married and move away from this area—anything could happen.'

She shook her head disbelievingly and said coldly, 'I don't think I've misunderstood you. Well, go ahead. Engage a full-time assistant. It will make life much easier for me—so much easier that I would be foolish to resign. Knowing that your hostility is completely unjustified, I've no doubt that I shall be able to survive.'

Staring at him defiantly, she saw that he was looking

at her with a curious expression in the depths of his eyes. Suddenly, surprisingly, he said, 'I suppose I could be wrong about you. You implied this morning that perhaps it was just as well Jane gave me up in favour of Derek. I've always imagined that it was pity for him that made her change her mind, but maybe that was only a sop to my pride. You said your reason for breaking it off with Derek was that you realised you had made a mistake. Was that a sudden decision on your part, or had that realisation come on gradually?'

Lisa stiffened. The memory of those days was still hurtful, and this man with his harsh, accusing manner was turning the knife in the wound — a wound that she thought had healed, but now, as a result of this insensitive probing, was becoming so painful that she could stand no more. Why, she thought bitterly, should she tell this stranger how, at the time, she had felt as though her heart would break? He only wanted to justify his abominable behaviour towards her. He deserved no explanation. At last she said in a voice that trembled a little, 'Do you really expect me to confide in you — give a day-by-day account of all that caused me to break off my engagement?' She drew a long, angry breath. 'You insulted me almost as soon as we met — called me horrible names — threatened me. . .' She broke off abruptly and went towards the door. 'Just leave me alone. That's all I ask.'

To her dismay he reached out and gripped her shoulder, forcing her round to face him.

'Don't touch me,' she said wildly. 'You're absolutely hateful and I loathe the sight of you.'

But his grip tightened. He said harshly, 'You're hiding something from me. Something I ought to know.'

'Take your hands off me.' She glared up at him. 'Stop asking me questions I refuse to answer.'

His deep-set eyes blazed back at her, his mouth tightened, and for a moment she felt a stab of alarm. Her fear must have shown in her face, because suddenly he released her.

'There's probably nothing to tell.' His mouth twisted scornfully. 'You're just trying to make me believe you had some justification for your behaviour towards my cousin. After all, I don't want to hear some trumped-up story guaranteed to make you look the injured party.'

She stared at him incredulously. So now he was calling her a liar. It was too much. Her resolution to stay on in the practice crumbled. It was not worth the trauma of fighting him. Her work would be affected. Every day would be unpleasant. Better to go now and have done with it. Before reflecting any further she said fiercely, 'You've gone too far. I can't possibly work here in this atmosphere. I resign. You can have the satisfaction of knowing you've got rid of me, and I'll have the satisfaction of never seeing you again.'

She saw his fist clench momentarily, then he said grimly, 'Running away again. That seems to be your speciality. But you can't just walk out, you know. You must give a month's notice at least.'

'I know that,' she said shortly. 'I'll speak to James this evening.'

Slamming the door behind her, she went quickly past an astonished Barbara and rushed up to her flat. There she paced the floor, trying to calm her thudding heart, and tears of mingled relief and regret filled her eyes. Impatiently she brushed them away. It was done now, and in one short day her whole life had changed. Just as it had changed a while back when Jane had come to see her a week before she was due to marry Derek.

CHAPTER TWO

AN HOUR later, her heart beating unpleasantly fast, Lisa rang James. His astonishment at the news she gave him was so great that he remained silent for what, to her, seemed an eternity. Then, at last, he said, 'But why? Why, for heaven's sake, do you want to leave? I thought you were happy here.'

His voice was troubled, and Lisa felt guilty and sad as she visualised his worried, kindly face. Swallowing hard to overcome the constriction in her throat, she said, 'It's very difficult to explain, but, to put it in a nutshell, Andrew Morland and I are simply not compatible as colleagues. I can't possibly stay on here.'

'Andrew? Why, you only met him today. . .' James paused. 'Or did you already know him? Is there something more you ought to tell me? My dear Lisa —— ' his voice was full of concern ' — come over here and have a talk about it. Angela and I may be able to help you.'

She had expected this, but, telling herself that a confidential talk was the last thing she wanted, she said, 'I'm sorry. I can't come this evening. Another time, perhaps. Meanwhile I'll write you a formal letter of resignation and send it to you as soon as possible.'

'Lisa! No. I won't accept it. There must be a way in which you and Andrew can settle your differences. Does he know you're threatening to resign?'

'I'm not threatening. I've quite decided, and yes, Andrew does know. I'm really very sorry, James, but there's nothing to be done about it.'

Just before she rang off she heard him say, 'Well, I'm

29

going to contact Andrew. I'm entitled to a better explanation than the one you've given me.'

Lisa's hands were shaking as she replaced the telephone, and she had to brush away tears of regret. Then, to her relief, her personal affairs were pushed into the background as a call came through for veterinary help.

An accident had occurred in a village about two miles away. A dog, obviously the victim of a hit-and-run car driver, had been found lying in a ditch, and the man who had discovered it had carried it back to his house. He gave his address and asked her to come as soon as possible as the dog was unconscious. A quick survey of the drugs in her case, a hurried call to Barbara to tell her where she was going, and Lisa was on her way.

It was a little difficult to find the lane in the dark, but as she turned the corner she saw a man standing in the lighted porch of a comfortable-looking creeper-clad house. Guiding her into the driveway, he opened the car door as she pulled up.

'Thank you for coming so quickly. I'm David Sinclair,' he said as he led her indoors, and, glancing at him quickly, Lisa liked what she saw. He was a man of medium height with a kind, serious face and a deep, pleasant voice. She guessed him to be round about forty, judging from the hint of grey in his dark almost black hair. Suddenly she found herself staring hard at a patch of blood on his shirt and, meeting her eyes, he said apologetically, 'I'm a bit messy, I'm afraid. That poor creature has some nasty cuts on his back. I just couldn't leave him there in that watery ditch. He's come round now while I've been watching over him.'

They had come into a large square oak-lined hall and, opening a door at the end, he showed her into the kitchen, where her patient lay covered by a blanket on a hastily improvised bed. Shrinking back at Lisa's touch, the large black mongrel whimpered pathetically, but allowed her to examine him without further protest.

At last she said, 'Well, he's been pretty lucky on the whole. Badly shocked, of course — I'll give him an injection for that right now — but no bones broken and, as far as I can tell at the moment, so sign of internal bleeding. I'll take him to the surgery, keep him under observation, and attend to those gashes on his back.' She paused. 'It was very good of you to bring him here, but you took a chance. He might have recovered consciousness and turned on you.'

David Sinclair smiled. 'He was very quiet. I don't think I've done him any harm, so don't scold, please.'

Lisa laughed. 'You deserve praise — not blame. Evidently you love dogs. Have you got one of your own?'

He shook his head. 'No. As a matter of fact I really prefer cats. They suit my way of life. I'm a writer — travel books — and naturally I'm away a lot, so my two cats go to a very good cattery not far from here. They're quite happy there and don't pine for me as a dog might.'

Lisa nodded as she filled a syringe, then, the injection given, she said, 'The sooner we get this casualty into the surgery, the better,' and was wrapping the blanket more closely round her patient when she heard a car pull up outside. Glancing up, she saw David Sinclair go to the window, then, with a quick word of excuse, he went out to the hall, leaving the kitchen door open. Suddenly she tensed up at the sound of a hated voice, and a moment later David came back, followed by Andrew. Before she could speak he said calmly,

'I've explained to Mr Sinclair that I don't like a woman going out at night in answer to a call from an unknown client.'

'He's quite right.' David smiled cheerfully. 'I'm glad he's so protective.'

Lisa said nothing, but with a quick glance at Andrew's stony expression she reflected wryly that 'protective' was hardly the word that applied to his attitude towards her. Then, as she finished wrapping up her patient, she said lightly,

'Well, since you're here, perhaps you would be good enough to put this dog into my car. I'm taking him back to the surgery.' Suddenly a thought occurred to her. 'Just a minute — there's a disc on his collar.' She pulled back the blanket. 'Yes — a telephone number and the owner's name. Johnson, Little Alton.'

David Sinclair said, 'I know the Johnson's — two middle-aged sisters who live in the village. They have a bookshop. I'll ring them and tell them what's happened.'

Andrew nodded. 'We'd better wait and see what they say. They might have their own vet and prefer him to take over the case.'

'The telephone is through here,' David said, and as he went out of the room Lisa said coldly,

'I'm quite used to doing night calls, you know. There was no need for you to be so — er — protective.' She paused and added mockingly, 'Come to think of it, that is the very last word to apply to your attitude towards me.'

His eyes glinted for a moment, then he said drily, 'Can you suggest a better one?'

She pondered, aware that she was asking for more trouble, but, determined that he should realise how much she disliked him, she said lightly, 'Aggressive — belligerent — vengeful. . . All more appropriate, don't you think?'

His mouth tightened, then he shrugged. 'The fact remains that I do not wish you to do any more night calls on your own. James agrees with me. We talked it over this morning.'

She stared at him in growing anger and said scornfully, 'The new broom sweeping everything clean. Well, you've succeeded in sweeping me out of the practice, so I shan't have to endure your petty restrictions much longer. I —— ' She stopped as David came back into the room. He glanced at them in momentary surprise at the sight of their flushed, angry faces, then he said,

'It's OK. I told them the whole story and they're concerned and grateful. Apparently they've only had the dog a short time — his name is Jasper — and they'd like you to attend to him. They'll call in at the surgery tomorrow morning. They haven't a car, so I'll drive them in.'

'Very kind of you,' Andrew said, and as he bent down to pick up the dog David drew Lisa to one side and said softly,

'Now that you know I'm not a dangerous type, would you consider coming out to dinner with me one evening?'

She hesitated, realising that she knew nothing about him, and uncomfortably aware that Andrew was within earshot. At last she said, 'How nice of you. Perhaps. . .' She smiled at him, obviously unwilling to commit herself. He seemed satisfied, however, and nodded.

'I'll be seeing you tomorrow morning. We'll fix up something then.'

Driving carefully with Jasper in the back of her car, Lisa saw with dismay that Andrew was following closely behind. He was obviously going to join her in the surgery. Now why on earth, she wondered irritably, did he want to do that? One would think she was incapable of doing anything on her own. Or was he perhaps going to lecture her about going out on night calls? Whatever he was contemplating, she determined to ignore him and not let her exasperation interfere with her concentration on her patient.

Pulling up outside the surgery, she found her fears confirmed. In a matter of moments he was standing beside her, and she frowned as he said briefly, 'I'll bring him in.'

She opened the back of the car in silence, then, as he picked up the dog, she said ungratefully, 'Barbara and I could have done it quite well. There was no need for you to come here.'

He said nothing, then, as she began to follow him, he half turned. 'You've left your car lights on.'

She gritted her teeth as she went back to extinguish them. Why, oh, why did he always manage to make her feel inadequate? He really was objectionable in every way, and any doubts that she had about leaving the practice were dispelled in the knowledge that she would find it increasingly hard to keep her temper in any future arguments. What, she wondered, would have been his attitude towards her if he had known nothing of her past history? Would he have been a friendly colleague? Unable to answer the question that had passed so rapidly through her mind, she went into the surgery and was relieved to find Barbara with everything ready for the casualty's reception, thus rendering Andrew's presence entirely unnecessary. Nevertheless he remained standing in the background as Lisa checked once more on the dog's condition. Having cleaned up the gashes on his back, she announced that she would let him sleep off the shock, and leave the operation till the morning. She turned to Barbara.

'He'll have to have a general anaesthetic, so would you mind coming in an hour before surgery time? Then he'll be done before his owners arrive.'

Barbara nodded, then asked doubtfully, 'Surely they won't expect to take him immediately, will they?'

Before Lisa could answer Andrew came forward. 'He

won't need a long-lasting anaesthetic. He'll be coming round by the time they arrive.'

Lisa drew a long breath, and gave him a glance so full of dislike that Barbara raised her eyebrows in surprise. She began hurriedly to clean the table as Andrew carried the patient to a recovery cage and Lisa angrily pulled off her overall and went to hang it up. Thanking Barbara and ignoring Andrew, she went out to put her car into the garage. She was just about to turn the ignition key when he came out and walked towards her. Flicking him a disdainful glance, she said sarcastically,

'Are you now going to tell me that it's not safe for a woman to put her car away in the dark?'

He gave an involuntary laugh — an attractive sound that made her almost want to join in — and for a moment she felt a pang of regret at the war-like atmosphere between them. Then, as he said nothing, she added impatiently,

'Do you mind moving away from my car? I want to go and fix myself something to eat.'

He stared. 'You haven't eaten yet? Come with me — there's a nice little restaurant I know where we could combine a meal with talking. Maybe we could clear the air between us and straighten out our differences.'

She gave him a quick, startled glance and shook her head.

'No, thank you.' She paused. 'There's nothing to talk over. You've built up this hostility between us, and a cosy little meal together isn't going to make me feel friendly towards you.'

Switching on the car lights, she put her hand once more on the ignition key, but with a swift movement he reached through the open window and gripped her wrist.

'We have to talk,' he said grimly. 'I know very well

that you're hiding something from me — something I ought to know — and that you're holding back in revenge for my first angry reaction when I realised who you were.' He paused. 'I'm right, aren't I?'

Conscious of the strength of his grasp, and knowing that to resist would only end in a ridiculous struggle, she took refuge in mockery.

'Goodness! How melodramatic! But yes — you're right. If you hadn't been so unpleasant to me from the first moment we met I might have told you what you want to know. But you wouldn't let me get a word in then, and only now are you beginning to realise that you behaved very badly. Well, you certainly did. You threatened me and forced me to resign from a job that I enjoyed until you arrived.' She drew a long, angry breath. 'So if you think I'm going to sit with you in a restaurant and tell you my innermost secrets over a meal and a glass of wine you're sadly mistaken. Now let go of my hand, please, and stand away from the car.'

For a moment his grip tightened so much that she winced, then abruptly he let her go and, as she shut the window, she caught a glimpse of his face. Even in the dim light she could see that his eyes were blazing with anger and his mouth was set in a grim line that totally belied his early, almost friendly approach. She opened the window again slightly and said scornfully,

'It was all an act, wasn't it? Your animosity towards me is too strong to hide for long. Well, it's reciprocated. I dislike you as much as you dislike me.'

Sliding her car into the garage, she sat for a few minutes trying to calm herself down. Then, when at last she got out and began to shut the doors, she saw the rear lights of his car going down the drive and heaved a long sigh of relief. Her euphoria lasted a long time. She cooked herself a meal and later, as she sat thoughtfully sipping a cup of coffee, she still felt elated. She had got her own back and, into the bargain, had shown him how contemptible she considered him to be. Then, suddenly, her triumphant mood faded. It was all so unnecessary. She could put an end to it immediately if she wished. She got up and began to walk restlessly about the room, wondering what best to do. At last she stopped her pacing and sat down to write her letter of resignation. This, to her dismay, proved to be much more difficult that she had imagined. A reason had to be given, and, put down on paper, incompatibility between Andrew and herself seemed weak and insubstantial. She could almost hear James saying that she ought to remember that first impressions were often wrong, that she mustn't act impulsively — there was no end to the arguments he would undoubtedly bring forward in his gentle, persuasive way. She sat pondering and frowning, and it was almost with relief that her troubled thoughts were interrupted by the sound of the telephone. But her frown deepened when, picking up the receiver, she found herself listening to James's wife.

Angela was plainly upset. 'James has told me of your threatened resignation. What on earth has come over you, Lisa.' Without waiting for Lisa's reply, she went on quickly, 'Look — we must have a talk. I might be able to help you. I've got some shopping to do tomorrow morning, so let's meet when you've finished surgery. I'll be in the coffee lounge at Lambtons. It's a good place to have a heart-to-heart.'

Reluctantly Lisa had to agree. She thought wryly that it was probably James's idea. He had a great dislike of unpleasant scenes and was all for a quiet life. Angela, with her forceful ways, would not hesitate to take up the cudgels on his behalf.

Half-an-hour later, her letter of resignation still unfinished, she was preparing to go to bed when the telephone rang again. This time it was David Sinclair, and his pleasant voice lifted her depression.

'I thought I'd ring now. It might be difficult tomorrow morning in the surgery. About this dinner with me. When will you be free?'

Thursday, her half-day, was agreed upon, and she went to bed with the feeling that someone outside the veterinary world might prove to be a friend with whom she could relax and forget her present troubles. Meeting David Sinclair had been the only good thing that had come out of this horrible day.

Next morning he arrived with the two ladies from the bookshop. In spite of the fact that Jasper had only been with them a short time he greeted them ecstatically, but was still rather unsteady on his feet after the anaesthetic, so David carried him out to the car while the two ladies fluttered around him. They had, they told Lisa, made all arrangements to have their fences repaired, Jasper would be guarded very carefully in future, and they promised to come back in ten days' time in order to have the stitches taken out.

Lisa smiled as she shut the door behind them. 'Jasper was supposed to be their guard dog,' she said, 'but it seems the roles are reversed.'

The two nurses laughed, and then Sally, glancing casually out of the window, exclaimed, 'Oh, look! That woman who claimed the lost cat yesterday seems to know Mr Sinclair. Chatting him up like anything. I thought she said she'd only been down here a few weeks.'

Unable to restrain her curiosity, Lisa went over to the window and was just in time to see David wave to Olivia Claydon as he drove away. She shrugged indifferently.

'I expect he's one of her brother's patients—she said she helped part-time in the reception office.'

'Well, she's coming in here,' said Sally. 'She's got a cat basket with her. Just as we thought we'd finished surgery. I suppose I'd better clean up this mess before she comes in.' It had been a busy surgery, with several unwilling patients who had shown their indignation by depositing unpleasant messes on the floor, and Sally made a face as she got down to her task.

'I must say,' she said resentfully, 'veterinary work isn't half as glamorous as it's made out to be on TV.'

Lisa laughed. 'The job of healing and caring for animals is bound to be smelly and unromantic at times.'

'That's what I'm learning fast,' said Sally. 'I wonder which is the more revolting — cleaning up after animals or humans, as hospital nurses have to.'

Barbara said drily, 'If you really want to find out you'd better go in for hospital nursing yourself.'

Sally sighed wistfully. 'All those lovely doctors. . .' Then, catching sight of the glint in Barbara's eyes, she turned hastily to Lisa. 'Shall I let Mrs Claydon in now?'

Lisa nodded. 'Actually it's twenty minutes after surgery time, but as she's here. . .'

Sally opened the waiting-room door, then exclaimed, 'She isn't here yet. I wonder. . .' She crossed over to the window. 'Goodness! Would you believe it? Andrew's car has just come in and she's standing talking to him now. She doesn't seem to miss a trick where men are concerned.'

'Sally!' Lisa rebuked her. 'You really must stop talking about our clients like this. Anyway, I expect she only wants a booster injection for Spot. It won't take long. You might as well start making the coffee.'

'Shall I put out a mug for Andrew?' Sally asked, then added pertly, 'Or aren't you and he on speaking terms?'

'Oh, shut up, Sally.' Barbara caught sight of the quick flush on Lisa's cheeks. 'Mind your own business. You're too curious by half.'

'It's only because I've come to the conclusion that people are more interesting than animals,' Sally retorted, and flounced off to put on the kettle, leaving the two other girls looking ruefully at each other.

Barbara sighed. 'I don't think she'll stay the course, you know. She was complaining yesterday that she could earn much more in an ordinary job.'

'No doubt about that——' Lisa shrugged '—but you don't do veterinary work for what you can get out of it in money terms. It's a caring profession. . .' She stopped and turned away to hid her confusion as she remembered the last time she had heard that phrase. Then, to her relief the waiting-room door opened and Olivia Claydon peered in.

'I know it's after surgery hours, but Andrew said it would be all right. I only want a booster injection for Spot.'

Subconsciously noting the use of Andrew's Christian name, Lisa nodded smilingly. 'Will you put the basket on the table, please? No need to take him out—just lift the lid and hold him firmly.'

It was done in a few moments, and as Olivia fastened the basket she looked up. 'Do you realise that David Sinclair is quite famous? I was talking to him outside—he's the travel writer whose books are always on the best-seller list.'

Lisa looked surprised and Barbara exclaimed, '*That* David Sinclair—goodness! I read his last book when I was on holiday. It was marvellous.'

Olivia nodded. 'My brother told me about him after David had been in for a check-up. He's a charmer, isn't he?'

Lisa suppressed a grin, but Barbara laughed outright. 'That's what you said about Andrew yesterday.'

Olivia shrugged. 'Well, it's true. They both are.' She turned to Lisa. 'Don't you agree with me?'

Lisa stiffened then said coolly, 'I really haven't given the matter any thought.' She paused. 'Have you got your cat's vaccination card? I must fill it in so that it keeps up to date.'

'Oh, dear, no. I think it must have been lost in the moving. Anyway, it doesn't matter much, does it?'

'Well, if you wanted to put Spot into a cattery at any time you'd have to produce it, so I'll make you out another one.'

She was filling it in when the outer door opened and Andrew came in and went into the dispensary. Then, rather to her dismay, Sally called, 'Would you like a coffee, Andrew? We're just going to have ours.'

He glanced round the partition. 'Yes, please. I'll join you in a minute.' He paused, then added, 'How about you, Mrs Claydon?'

'Oh, call me Olivia, please. Yes, I'd love a coffee.' She flashed him a brilliant smile. 'I must say I like this veterinary atmosphere rather better than that at the health centre. It's so much more relaxed.'

She seated herself at the table as Sally began to pour out. Andrew sat down beside her, and for a moment Lisa hesitated, longing to take her coffee upstairs to her flat. Then, realising it would look too obvious, she sat down reluctantly. Turning to her, Andrew said coolly,

'When we've finished, will you come into the office, please? I've been talking to James and ——'

'Oh, goodness! That reminds me. . .' Lisa got up quickly. 'I've promised to meet Angela for coffee. I'm sorry, but I must go. I'm late as it is.' She turned to Barbara. 'You can get me at Lambtons if anything urgent comes in.'

Hurriedly she went to hang up her overall, and when she came back she found Andrew holding the door open for her. He said quietly,

'James and I have a proposition to put to you, and I

rather wanted to tell you myself, but I expect Angela will spill the beans. Mind you, we've only just thought it out, so it will have to be fully discussed.'

Lisa stared. 'A proposition? I don't think. . .' She shrugged, glanced pointedly at her watch. 'Anyway, I must go. Goodbye, all.'

As she went out to her car she thought wryly, Well, at least I've been warned. They've hatched up some scheme between them, but I don't see that it can make any difference to the fact that Andrew and I dislike each other too much to work together amicably. I must keep that in mind and not allow myself to be persuaded to agree to something I might regret later. Armed with this resolution, she went quickly into Lambtons and up to the coffee lounge.

Angela Carter, who was plump, with greying hair, had a pretty face with a gentle smile which belied a very forceful character. She had secured a table in a quiet corner. Sitting down, Lisa hardly had time to settle herself before she said briskly, 'Now, my dear, what's all this nonsense about your leaving us?'

'It's not nonsense,' said Lisa calmly. 'How much has James told you?'

'All he knows, which isn't much. Something about your not being able to get on with Andrew.' She paused, poured the coffee, then passed over a plate of luscious-looking pastries. 'Oh, come on. One won't hurt you. It will be embarrassing for me if you sit there watching me being greedy.'

Lisa laughed as she chose a chocolate eclair. 'My favourite,' she said, and Angela nodded approvingly, then returned to the fray.

'Now you simply must tell me why you dislike Andrew so much. James said you had only met him for the first time yesterday, but I'm sure that's wrong. You couldn't have made such a drastic decision on the strength of a few minutes' conversation. So what's the story? Have you had an affair with him in the past?'

Lisa's face flamed at the blunt question. Resentfully she said, 'Good lord, no! It's nothing like that.' She paused. It was obvious that some kind of explanation was called for, or Angela would build up an imaginary story that would make matters infinitely worse. 'Look,' she said at last, 'Andrew and I started off on the wrong foot. He was very rude to me and I lost my temper. That sounds simple, but it isn't. We both said things that were — well — unforgivable and unforgettable.' She paused, then added firmly, 'I meant it. I can't possibly work with him.'

There was a long silence. Angela, for once, seemed lost for words. At last, recovering herself, she said slowly, 'You're just giving me the bare bones of the situation. James said he got the same impression from Andrew, who was equally evasive. Be fair to us, Lisa. We deserve a little more information. You've been with us for eighteen months. You've worked for us loyally and we're very fond of you. So much so that James is about to offer you a partnership now. He's decided to retire completely, and naturally wants to leave the practice in good hands. Yours and Andrew's. It would be a marvellous thing for you. Not many girls get such a chance so young.'

Lisa's eyes widened in astonishment. 'So soon? James is going to give up completely?'

Angela nodded. 'Yes. Rather earlier than he planned, but his heart has been playing up lately. His doctor says that struggling with farm animals is absolutely out, and you know he's never cared for small-animal work.' She paused, seeing the doubt on Lisa's face. 'If you're wondering about the financial side, then you can relax. Andrew is buying his share, but James says you've worked up the small animal surgery from almost nothing, so he would like to give you your partnership as a reward.' She shook her head as she saw Lisa stiffen. 'No, this isn't bribery. He always meant to give you a half-share, only it's come a little sooner than he planned because of his health. Now you must be equally generous with us. Tell me the whole story — I'm sure there's much more behind your antagonism towards Andrew than a few hasty words spoken in anger. Besides, it's not like you to lose your temper, especially with someone you'd only just met, and, as for Andrew — it's quite unbelievable.'

Lisa drew a long breath. Things had taken an unexpected turn, and reluctantly she realised she must respond by giving some sort of explanation. Slowly and carefully she described how Andrew had reacted when he'd discovered her identity. She told how taken aback she had been at his violent and scornful abuse, how she had been unable to justify herself, and ended by quoting his dramatic statement that she had ruined his life because the girl he loved had married Derek instead. 'Unfortunately,' she added, 'he didn't tell me that till later, when I'd already lost my temper at what I considered to be his exaggerated loyalty to his cousin.'

Angela looked at her blankly for a full minute, then, putting down her coffee-cup, she leant forward.

'I suppose I shouldn't ask this, but I'm going to nevertheless, because I feel that it must have some bearing on the situation — why *did* you break off your wedding plans at the last minute?'

Lisa frowned and shook her head. 'I don't think——' She stopped as Angela put up her hand.

'Let me guess. Would it have been something you found out about your fiancé? Was he having an affair with another woman — this girl that Andrew loved?'

Lisa nodded helplessly, and Angela shrugged dismissively.

'Well, that's not the end of the world nowadays, so why did you react in such a dramatic fashion? Why didn't you have it out with him — give him another chance? I should have thought that, if you really loved him, you would have been prepared to forgive him.'

Lisa's face clouded and she sighed resignedly. It was useless to try and hold back anything from Angela. She smiled ruefully.

'All right. I'll tell you, but in strict confidence. This girl came to see me a week before the wedding and said she was pregnant with Derek's baby. I'd never met her before, and at first I didn't believe her. Then she gave me details of the affair — the times they had spent together and so on. It all linked up, so finally I went straight to Derek. I didn't tell him she was pregnant — I left that to her to do. In any case, there was no need, because as soon as I charged him with having an affair with Jane he admitted it and said that, although he was fond of me, he really wanted to marry Jane but hadn't had the courage to tell me.' Lisa paused. 'Well, I still loved him.' She hesitated again. 'At least I thought I did, so I let him go, gave it out that I'd changed my mind at the last minute. What else could I do?'

Angela's face softened. She said pityingly, 'Poor Lisa. What a sad experience. In a way it was a good thing that your parents. . .'

Lisa nodded. 'Yes. I was almost glad they had been killed in that car crash.' She swallowed hard, then went on, 'Well, I did the obvious thing — packed in my job as assistant vet in our local practice and came down here. . .far enough away to avoid any contact with the past.'

'One thing puzzles me.' Angela frowned. 'Why have you put up with all this unpleasantness from Andrew? Why let him misjudge you like this?'

Lisa hesitated. Certainly her silence seemed foolish,

a self-imposed martyrdom for which there was no reasonable explanation.

'Really, Lisa——' Angela had seen her indecision '—you must be mad. You've always been so level-headed and so sensible, but now you're behaving like some silly girl in a soap opera.'

Lisa's face reddened. An angry retort rose to her lips, then, catching sight of the kindly concern in the older woman's face, she stayed silent. It was true, she acknowledged ruefully to herself. Andrew's unjustified attack must have knocked her off balance, and she was behaving like an idiot. Reaching out, she took Angela's hand and said slowly,

'You're right. You've brought me to my senses. I'll do what you say and tell him the truth as soon as possible.'

Driving back to the surgery, Lisa felt as though a load had been lifted from her shoulders. The prospect of an early partnership filled her with pleasant anticipation and a feeling of achievement in her professional life. She must now find an opportunity to put things straight with Andrew. It wouldn't be easy, but it had to be done. Mentally she began to rehearse her explanation, but a vision of his grim face made her heart beat nervously. Although she knew she was not at fault—in fact he was the one who would have to apologise for misjudging her so hastily—nevertheless she felt it was going to be a very unpleasant ordeal.

CHAPTER THREE

BACK at the surgery, Lisa found the two nurses deep in conversation. Sally looked up, her pretty face alight with laughter.

'You should have been here, Lisa. Olivia was making up to Andrew as hard as she could, and it was side-splitting to see the way in which he dodged all her questions. Well, nearly all. She managed to find out that he isn't involved with anyone at present — admittedly he was a bit vague on that subject, but it seemed to satisfy her — then when he said he knew this part of the country well she tried to get him to show her the local beauty spots. When he said he simply didn't have the time she suggested he could take her out on his rounds sometimes, and he looked so horrified at that that she had to pretend she was joking.' Catching sight of the expression on Lisa's face, Sally shrugged. 'OK, so you're not interested, but there's one more thing. Just before she left, Olivia said she and her brother were going to give a house-warming party to which she hoped we'd all come.' She paused. 'Well, I'm certainly going. I've got a thing about doctors, and there are bound to be several there.'

Barbara smiled sardonically and turned to Lisa. 'The fact that Sally already has a boyfriend doesn't seem to matter, does it?'

Sally shrugged scornfully. 'You're too stuffy for words. It's a good thing to have several strings to one's bow. Oh, and David Sinclair has promised to go.' She paused. 'She couldn't pin Andrew down though. He was very guarded — said if he were free he'd be

47

delighted but she had to remember that a vet was on twenty-four-hour call, but she knew that was a bit feeble and said she looked forward to seeing us all. She'd fix the date later.'

'Well, she won't see me,' said Barbara, 'so I'll be able to deal with any messages that come in.'

Sally looked shocked. 'You must be mad — it sounds like a good party.' She turned to Lisa. 'There's no need for anyone to stay here, is there? The phone can be transferred.'

'I know that,' Barbara said coolly, 'but you seem to forget that I'm engaged, and I don't care to go to a party without George.'

Interrupted by the telephone, Lisa was glad to abandon the subject, and, after listening for a few moments, she turned back to Barbara.

'That was Andrew. He's picked up an abandoned dog on the motorway. He's bringing it in now.'

A quarter of an hour later Andrew placed a sad little mongrel on the table, exhausted and frightened. The expression in his eyes was heart-rending.

Andrew said grimly, 'He must have run for miles after the car containing his cruel owners. Look at the state of his feet.' He paused, stroking the rough, neglected coat. 'A couple of nasty sores here on his back — God, I'd like to get my hands on the brute who did that.'

There was silence for a while as they contemplated the mournful little animal, then Lisa said, 'I think a bath and then a meal, don't you? Then we'll have to decide what to do with him.'

When the dog had been bathed and his sores dressed, Sally placed a bowl of dog food down and the little mongrel set to as though he had been starved for days. Putting down the telephone receiver, Andrew said, 'The police have given us a free hand — said if we could

find the dog a good home they'd be glad. There's no
hope of catching the owner — this kind of thing is
happening all the time.'

Lisa frowned as she pondered the problem, then
suddenly her face brightened. She turned to Barbara.
'Remember Mr Barrett? Do you think. . .?'

She left the question unfinished, as Barbara was
already searching for the old man's telephone number.
A few minutes later Lisa went to the telephone and
came back smiling.

'He's overjoyed. He says he'll be here in about thirty
minutes. A neighbour will give him a lift in his car.'
Catching sight of Andrew's raised eyebrows, she said,
'It's OK. Mr Barrett will take good care of your
forsaken dog. We put his old one to sleep yesterday,
and he says he was wondering how he could live without
it. He was so overjoyed that I didn't get the chance to
describe his new pet.'

There was silence for a few moments as they studied
the little mongrel carefully, then Andrew said, 'About
a year old, I should say. Very mixed parentage — he's
no beauty, but he's got fine expressive eyes full of
intelligence. He'll reward your Mr Barrett with years of
love and devotion.'

Barbara laughed. 'Mixed parentage all right. That's
putting it mildly. Usually one can tell a little of a
mongrel's ancestry, but this one is a complete mystery.'
She paused. 'It reminds me of my cousin's new baby.
Both parents are dark, but their baby's hair is flaming
red. The jokes the poor mother has to put up with are
unbelievable.'

A sudden thought flashed like lightning across Lisa's
brain. It was an alarming thought. The baby that was
supposed to be Derek's — could it be that Jane had
been lying? Might it not be Andrew's child? It was said
that he had been in Canada for three months — Jane

might well have discovered she was pregnant as the result of an affair with him but decided Derek, who was a very prosperous businessman with a great financial future, would be a better bet when it came to marriage. It was true that Jane had had an affair with Derek, but she might also have had one with Andrew. Suddenly Lisa saw where her thoughts were all leading. Impossible now to tell Andrew the reason why she had abandoned her marriage plans with his cousin. It was only to be supposed that Andrew would one day visit Derek, with whom he was presumably on good terms. Both Jane and Derek had green eyes — beautiful in Jane's case, and the only redeeming feature in Derek's rather nondescript face. If their baby bore no resemblance to its parents, it would probably not occur to Andrew that the baby might be his, but if he knew the whole unhappy story, then, depending on the relationship he had had with the girl he loved, then he might become suspicious. Although Lisa held no brief for Jane, she had no wish to break up Derek's marriage.

At that moment her own telephone rang, and after listening for a few moments she handed the receiver to Andrew. He seemed surprised as he took down the message, then, replacing the instrument, he turned to Lisa.

'An interesting case. Would you like to come with me?'

She hesitated then said, 'Well, if you think I can help, though I'm afraid I'm rather rusty where large animals are concerned.'

'All the more reason why you should do some work on farms, but this is nothing to do with the usual cows or pigs. It's to do with pheasants. Are you interested?'

'Pheasants? Goodness! Of course I am.' And, turning to Barbara and Sally, she said, 'I'll leave you in charge. If anything urgent should come in, ring through on

Andrew's car phone.' Picking up her case, she continued, 'I'll have to take my car in case I'm wanted here.'

'No need for that,' Andrew said easily. 'I can drive you back.'

'But you might have another call——'

'Oh, don't quibble. I've told you, I'll get you back if necessary,' he said impatiently and, going to the door, he added, 'I'll wait outside for you.'

A few words to the two girls then she went to join him, feeling rather as though she had been dragooned into accompanying him. All the same, she was pleased to get out of the groove of small-animal practice and widen her experience.

For the first few minutes they sat in silence, then Andrew said, 'Mr Hampton over at Ridge Farm runs a shooting syndicate—buys in poults and rears them for the shoot. Now the gamekeeper—Bill Watson—has asked Mr Hampton to call me in to try and solve a problem. I don't know any more than that. Some kind of game-bird disease, I suppose.'

'Do you think it might be coccidiosis?'

He shook his head. 'I asked him that, but he said no. All the same, we must take everything into account when we see them.'

The way in which Andrew was including her in the case was pleasing, and enabled Lisa to put aside her personal doubts and fears, and conversation between them became easy and relaxed. Driving away from the Downs into more wooded country, Andrew said,

'This farm is the furthest out from our practice area. Have you ever been out this way?'

'I've passed through, but I've never done any farm work here——' Lisa paused '—or anywhere else for that matter. I'm strictly small-animal practice, which I sometimes regret, especially on a day like this.'

It was indeed a beautiful day. The yellow and gold of early autumn leaves on the trees stood against a brilliant blue sky, and as Andrew turned down a lane leading to the farm a magnificent cock pheasant rose from the hedge with a loud cry.

'That one looks healthy enough,' Lisa said, watching the colourful bird fly out to a neighbouring wood.

'Ah, yes. He's one that has survived the guns of previous years.' Andrew paused. 'What are your views on game shooting?'

'Well. . .' Lisa hesitated. 'I hate the idea, but I realise that if game birds weren't reared for shooting it wouldn't be long before they disappeared from our countryside.'

Andrew nodded. 'No good shooting syndicate worth its name ever kills all the birds it rears.' He drew up outside the farmhouse and got out. 'I'll just go and tell Mr Hampton that we're on our way to the game-keeper's cottage.'

He was back in a few minutes, and they then drove over a farm track for about a mile into the woods. There, in a clearing, he pulled up outside a picturesque cottage surrounded by a neat garden. A black Labrador and a large English springer spaniel lay basking in the autumnal sun, but at the sight of the car they rose quickly. It would obviously be foolish to open the gate and walk towards them, so Andrew remained in his seat and gave a toot on the horn. Almost immediately a sturdy-looking man in his forties emerged, and the dogs relaxed as their master greeted his visitors in friendly fashion. After being introduced to Lisa he said, 'Two heads are better than one.' Turning to Andrew, he added, 'Four more birds dead this morning. It's very worrying.'

As they walked with him into the wood he said in answer to Lisa's question. 'It's like this: I've got two flocks of pheasants—two thousand birds in all—and they were reared together until about six weeks of age. Then they were transferred to release pens—one lot in that area over there. The other thousand are in this walled plot we're coming to. The trouble began about a fortnight ago. Several birds were seen limping, and in a week eighty more were affected. About a hundred now, and some have died.' He paused. 'I've got three for you to examine. They're in this hut.'

On a table inside three young cock pheasants lay still as the keeper went up to them, but as soon as Andrew and Lisa approached they flapped their wings.

'That's about the only movement they're capable of making,' said the keeper. 'See the swelling on the tendon just above the hock. . .?' He held one of the birds gently but firmly, and Andrew touched the puffy area.

'Yes, it can be palpatated,' he said. 'There's fluid there and an infection which is spreading.' He drew Lisa forward. 'What do you think?'

She examined the bird, then looked up. 'It seems to me that an injury has occurred to the feet and it's there that the infection gets in. But what kind of injury?' She paused. 'Could we have a look round the release pen?'

Once there they searched for nails or broken glass, then Lisa looked up quickly when Andrew asked, 'These trees growing here—what are they? A sort of spruce?'

'Norway spruce.' The keeper nodded. 'Those small branches were cut from the trunks in the summer. Do you reckon. . .?' He stooped as Andrew was doing, and then as they stood upright they frowned at the sharp, splintery pieces in their hands.

The keeper spoke slowly. 'It's possible and, of course, when there's rivalry between the male birds that would contribute to the damage.'

'Nice work,' Andrew said softly to Lisa and, for a moment, she glowed with pleasure. He went on, 'I'd better send some dead birds to the Veterinary Investigation Centre to ascertain exactly what the infection is. Meantime, this flock must be kept isolated from the others. For treatment I'll give tetracycline medication. You can put it in their drinking water, and if it's a staphylococcal infection that should do the trick. And, of course, those bits of Norway spruce must be completely cleared away.'

Driving back, they discussed the case for a while and Lisa said, 'I'm surprised the gamekeeper didn't discover those sharp splinters himself.'

'Well, he's quite inexperienced. Mr Hampton told me it's his first job as a full-time gamekeeper. Also of course he's like so many people nowadays — they never look out for simple causes; everything has to be a virus, the more mysterious the better.' Andrew laughed. 'I've enjoyed this trip, have you?'

'Very much. I'm so glad you asked me to come.'

He gave her a quick sideways glance. 'We make a good professional partnership, don't you think?'·

It was undeniable, and Lisa nodded, then, hurriedly changing the subject, she said, 'You know, I find it difficult to understand how a gamekeeper can bear to rear those birds from chicks and look after them so well that they run up to him and even take food from his hands. Then he organises the shoot and sees them shot down in full flight.'

'I know.' Andrew nodded sympathetically. 'It's a question I've often asked myself. Of course it's a job that involves killing: he has to shoot vermin — they have to be kept down. But a good keeper should be a naturalist and know how to preserve the balance of nature.' He paused, then added slowly, 'Actually, when I was in my late teens, I used to go round with a

gamekeeper who was an expert shot and was praised by
my uncle, who was his employer, for the way he kept
the fox population down and preserved the game birds.
Then one day when I was out with him I found myself
staring straight into a fox's eyes. So beautiful. Wild,
yes, but completely innocent. Like a dog's eyes. It was
that innocence that got to me. I gave up shooting from
that moment.'

A lump formed in Lisa's throat. This was something
she could understand and with which she could identify.
Impulsively she put her hand on his shoulder in a quick
gesture of sympathy. Then, as her hand dropped, he
took his left one off the gear lever and covered her
fingers for a few seconds.

Her silence as they drove along did not seem to
trouble Andrew. Like her, he appeared lost in thought,
and he only spoke when he pulled up outside the
surgery.

Smiling down at her as she got out of the car, he said,
'We must go out together more often.'

Evening surgery was so busy that all Lisa's thoughts
were concentrated on her work. Cats and dogs succeeded each other in what seemed a never-ending
procession. Some of their needs were routine — injec-
tions against killer diseases, skin troubles, behaviour
problems and the inevitable troubles of old age. Guinea
pigs, gerbils and tame rabbits made for a little variety
and, occasionally, there were cases that required understanding of human nature. Here Lisa was at her tactful
best. Neurotic owners well on the way to transforming
perfectly well-balanced animals into shivering nervous
wrecks had to be persuaded that their over-protective
behaviour was harmful to their pets, and happy-go-
lucky clients who bought puppies as toys for their
children were difficult to convince that their treatment

caused suffering and sometimes real cruelty to their helpless pets. Then there were the owners who grumbled at the charges made for treatment and who seemed to think that veterinary surgeons were all included in the National Health Service and thought that everything should be free. One of the clients in this category, who had arrived in a large car and was wearing expensive clothes, had argued so unpleasantly about his bill that, when at last he left, Lisa felt drained and exhausted. Then, as she saw Barbara and Sally glancing anxiously at their watches, she pulled herself together.

'You two had better go — don't bother about clearing up. I'm in no hurry, so I'll do it this evening.'

She worked swiftly, and at last, with a final survey of the room, she decided to ring Angela. But, standing with the instrument in her hand, she hesitated. James and his wife would most probably be together, and Angela might well lose her temper and, forgetting that she was bound to secrecy, tell the whole story to her husband. Despairingly she put the telephone back on its hook. How awful it was to be so indecisive — to be constantly changing her mind. She had never been like this before. Hitherto the way ahead had always been plainly marked out, but now she hardly knew which road to take. At last she decided to write her formal letter of resignation to James and, in a separate one to Angela, tell her that another problem had arisen which necessitated breaking her promise to divulge everything to Andrew. After that she must stay firm and leave quietly when her month's notice had expired.

She was up in her flat when the telephone rang and, on hearing Andrew's voice, she stiffened automatically. What now, she wondered — more trouble? Then, as his words penetrated, her eyes widened in surprise.

'Lisa — I need your professional help. My old dog has reached the end of the road. I have to put him to sleep, but——' he stopped and she heard him draw a long, harsh breath '—I find I simply cannot do it myself. Will you come to my house, please, as soon as possible? I want him to go peacefully in his home surroundings.' He paused, then, as though sensing her uncertainty, he added, 'I'm asking your help as one vet to another.'

'Of course. I'll come right away.' Lisa replaced the telephone and stood for a moment, deep in thought. It was a situation that she understood and with which she sympathised, but it was nevertheless embarrassing. She shrugged her shoulders. Of course he was right.

She had no time to study the exterior of his house, as he came out to meet her as soon as she turned into the driveway, but she got a quick impression of a large, imposing entrance as he led her indoors. Seen in his home surroundings, it was once again difficult to remember that he was her avowed enemy. This was a man who was sick at heart at the prospect of losing an old and dearly loved friend, and instinctively she felt the need to comfort him in his pain.

He turned to look at her as they passed down a large hall.

'I've filled a syringe and approached Ben twice, but each time my hand has trembled so much that. . .'

He shook his head, as though bewildered at his weakness and Lisa said quickly, 'Please don't despise yourself. I understand only too well.' She paused and sighed. 'Dogs have such a short life. That's one reason why I haven't got one myself. When our old family dog died I felt I couldn't stand that heartbreak again.'

He stared at incredulously. 'I find that inexplicable. You're denying yourself years and years of love and devotion because you're afraid of getting hurt, quite apart from the fact that you can give a helpless animal a good life when so many of them suffer from human cruelty.'

Lisa flushed hotly, then, unable to endure his searching, puzzled gaze, she said, 'Let's go and see to your Ben.'

The springer spaniel tried to get to his feet as his master approached, and his sad old eyes were full of appeal as the effort proved too much for him. Andrew said quietly, 'It's all right, old boy. You stay there.' Going down on his knees, he cradled the tired head in his arms and, half turning, he said in a broken voice, 'The syringe is on the table.'

She picked it up and stood waiting as he looked deep into the dim, loving eyes and murmured soothingly in a way that brought a painful lump into her throat. At last he said, 'Now, please.'

In a very short time it was all over, and as Andrew began to rise to his feet she said quickly, 'Don't get up. I'll see myself out.'

She was halfway down the hall when he came up behind her. Turning, she saw that his face was haggard with grief, and in quick sympathy she said, 'He went so peacefully with you holding him. A quiet end to a long, happy life.'

Unexpectedly he put his hand on her shoulder. 'Thank you for being so understanding,' he said.

Driving the short distance back to her flat, she still felt the impress of his hand, and the look of gratitude in the deep-set hazel eyes was faintly disturbing. He was a strange man — a man of strong emotions, quick to anger, obstinate and proud, yet not too proud to acknowledge his weakness when it came to putting an end to his beloved dog's life. Reluctantly she conceded that if there had been no friction between them she would have found him very likeable indeed.

Puzzled she went to sleep that night hoping that her subconscious mind would sort things out and supply her with a solution in the morning.

But when the alarm clock woke her she was still as worried as ever until, after a bracing shower, she managed to pull herself together. What will be, will be, she told herself fatalistically, and she must let events take their course.

Surgery that morning was not very busy, and with no operations to do, and the nurses working in the recovery-room, Lisa sat drinking her coffee alone. Gradually her calm acceptance of her dilemma faded as she faced up to the fact that she must come to a decision soon. Pushing her coffee aside, she put her elbows on the table and buried her face in her hands. She was so absorbed in her worried thoughts that the sound of the outer door opening made no impression on her, and it was only when she heard Andrew's voice that she looked up in alarm. He was standing staring down at her, and there was real concern in his face.

'What's wrong? Aren't you well, Lisa?'

She stood up quickly. 'No — no — I'm perfectly OK. I was just. . .well, I was just relaxing.'

'Hmm.' He looked at her doubtfully, then smiled a little grimly. 'This seems to be the opportunity I've been seeking. We need to talk. I'll just make myself a coffee.'

Frowning, she said, 'Actually I've finished mine and I've got some paperwork to do. I really haven't time to —'

'Oh, yes, you have,' he said calmly. 'Sit down again — this is important.'

Reluctantly she waited until he brought his coffee to the table, then she said rather nervously, 'This talk — is it about work? Something professional?'

'Yes and no,' he said. 'In the first instance I want to thank you again for your help and understanding last night. It was a real indication to me that we could work together as partners very successfully.' He paused.

'However, in order to achieve this, there must be no cause for friction between us — no hidden resentment that could do damage to our work. By that I mean the stress of constant quarrelling and lack of trust.' He stopped and gazed at her meaningly and, determined not to show her apprehension, she looked back at him steadily but stayed silent.

'You do know what I'm getting at, don't you?' he asked impatiently, and she knew she had no option but to answer.

'Not really,' she said evasively, 'but perhaps I'm being obtuse. Are you apologising for the beastly things you've said to me? If so, you will have to be more explicit.'

He shook his head irritably. 'No, I'm not apologising again.' He paused, and she saw his face redden. 'Oh, all right! I admit I did go too far. But what I'm trying to say——' He broke off abruptly as the outer door opened, and a second later Angela came into the room.

He muttered something under his breath, but recovered quickly.

'Good lord! What a pleasant surprise.'

Lisa smiled with relief. 'Come and have a cup of coffee with us.'

Angela hesitated. 'I'd better not. I haven't much time.' She nodded towards the office. 'I've just come to get some papers for James.' Then, glancing from one to the other, she said bluntly, 'So you've made up your differences. What a good thing. Now we can go ahead as planned.'

Confused, Lisa could find no words with which to disillusion her, but Andrew said coolly, 'We're merely having a professional discussion.'

Angela frowned. 'If that is meant to imply that the situation between you hasn't changed, then I can only suppose that you, Lisa, have not yet told Andrew, as you assured me you would.'

'Told me what?' Andrew asked sharply, but Angela shook her head. 'It's not up to me. Ask her yourself.'

Going into the office, she opened a drawer in the desk, pulled out a packet of papers, and with a brief goodbye she was gone.

Unable to bear the now oppressive silence, Lisa got up and began to wash her coffee-mug. Suddenly she felt her shoulders gripped, and was so startled that she dropped the mug into the sink.

'For goodness' sake!' she protested angrily. 'Look what you've made me do. It's broken.' Furiously she tried to shake him off, but he pulled her round to face him.

'If you've told Angela something you ought to have told me, then I must know. Come on. Out with it.'

Lisa glared up at him, her eyes blazing with anger at his rough treatment. This, she thought bitterly, is because I was stupid enough to confide in Angela. I might have known she'd blurt it out. Aloud she said flatly, 'Please take your hands off me.'

He spoke through clenched teeth. 'I won't let you go until you tell me.'

In spite of her thudding heart she said defiantly, 'Then we'll stay here till someone else comes in.'

The muscles tightened round his lips, and he looked so grim that she felt a momentary stab of fear. Recovering herself quickly, she said mockingly, 'Stop acting so childishly.'

His eyes glinted. 'I'm not feeling the least bit childish, and to prove it. . .' Suddenly his arms went right round her, enclosing her in a grip of steel.

Gasping, she said, 'Let me go. Let me ——' But his lips came down on hers and stifled her furious protest. Her heart seemed to stand still, and when, at last, he lifted his head she was struggling for breath and angry tears were burning at the back of her eyes.

'How dare you?' she raged. 'Are you out of your mind?'

He stared down at her, brooding and speculative, then he said harshly, 'I think I must be.'

Abruptly he let her go, and a moment later the door slammed behind him. Drawing a long, deep breath, Lisa pulled out a chair and sat down, staring unseeingly ahead. She tried to steady her racing heart, but the feel of his lips on hers in that passionate kiss refused to go away. It was a full minute before she realised that the telephone was ringing, and her hand was still shaking as she picked up the receiver.

Angela's voice brought reality back, and as she listened she frowned and shook her head despondently.

'Dinner tomorrow evening,' said Angela firmly. 'James wants to get things settled. Be here about seven-thirty — is that OK?'

Suddenly Lisa remembered. Tomorrow — her half-day and her date with David Sinclair. She said quickly, 'I'm sorry Angela. I really can't manage tomorrow evening. I'm engaged — dinner with a friend.'

There was a short silence, then Angela said coldly, 'Lisa, this is important. James is extremely agitated at the way things are, and you will be causing him even more stress if you refuse to come. You must put off your date.'

Lisa sighed with exasperation. It was a command, and she had no option. As soon as she had reluctantly accepted she replaced the receiver and began to search for David's number. The sound of his calm voice helped to soothe her ruffled temper, and the cheerful way in which he accepted her explanation made her feel that here was a friend in whom she could trust.

'Don't worry. I haven't booked a table yet. May I fix it for — say — Saturday evening?'

Somehow she wanted to refuse altogether, but that was impossible.

'Yes,' she said, 'that will be fine.'

'OK,' he said easily, 'I'll look forward to it.'

Sighing, Lisa replaced the receiver and stood frowning as she tried to imagine what Angela's dinner party would be like. James obviously wanted to get things settled, so that would mean giving a definitive yes or no to his offer of a partnership. Well, it would just have to be no, and she must stick firmly to the reason she had given. She would not, could not, work alongside Andrew, even as an assistant, and to bind herself to a partnership with him was unthinkable. The bond of sympathy which had seemed to unite them when she had put his dog to sleep had been effectively broken by the way in which he had tried to force her to talk about the past. His furious kiss had degraded her so much that she felt she never wanted to speak to him again, and she resolved that once she had settled things with James she would keep well away from Andrew Morland right up to the time she left the practice.

CHAPTER FOUR

UNEASY and preoccupied with the thought of what lay ahead, Lisa got through the rest of Wednesday in a mood of deep depression. It was only when, towards the end of evening surgery, she found herself hesitating over the treatment of a relatively simple case that she realised how much her worries were intruding into her professional life. Hurriedly she pulled herself together, only to feel her heart sink again when Barbara said, 'Andrew's car has just driven in. He's carrying something — a cat, I think.'

A moment later he came in, smiling wryly. 'Olivia Claydon's cat. I'll put it in the recovery-room. Nothing wrong with it except an excess of wanderlust. I found it on Mr Baker's farm — that's about two miles away. I took it round to her house, but no one's there. Perhaps one of you wouldn't mind giving her a ring later.' He turned on the way out. 'By the way, Lisa, as it's your half-day tomorrow I'll take evening surgery. Have you any particular problems or instructions?'

She said distantly, 'If anything crops up I'll leave full details for you.'

'Right. I've warned Angela that I may be a little late. She said seven-thirty, but I may not get there much before eight.' The dismay she felt must have shown on her face, for he added drily, 'Oh, yes. I have to be there as well.'

The rest of the day passed uneventfully, and it was only the following morning during the coffee break that she realised her preoccupied manner was noticeable to the nurses. Meeting Barbara's puzzled look, she said, 'Oh, sorry — I was far away. What did you ask?'

Barbara said sympathetically, 'You look as though you'd got the troubles of the world on your shoulders. Anything we can do to help?'

With difficulty Lisa managed a laugh. 'Actually there's nothing important on my mind. It's probably the prospect of having to go to dinner with James and Angela that's making me look rather depressed. Andrew will be there too as it's to do with the future of the practice. I expect it will be pretty boring.'

She was pleased with the way she had staved off all curiosity, and the conversation took a different turn until Sally said suddenly, 'Listen — that wretched cat is being sick. How revolting!' She made no attempt to go and investigate, and it was Barbara who began cleaning up the mess while Lisa examined the patient.

'Nothing wrong as far as I can tell.' She made a face as she surveyed the contents of its stomach. 'I think he's been eating too many mice, by the look of things.'

Barbara laughed, but suddenly Sally turned white and rushed over to the sink. Lisa stared and exclaimed,

'Good heavens! What's wrong? You've seen animals being sick before — why this sudden squeamishness?' Then as Sally burst into tears she added compassionately, 'Come and sit down. Leave your coffee — a cup of tea will make you feel better.'

Sally said nothing, but Barbara, looking rather grim, refilled the kettle, and a few minutes later Sally drew a long breath and said in a low voice, 'I feel awful. I think I'm pregnant.'

Lisa gasped, but Barbara showed no surprise. 'I was beginning to wonder,' she said calmly. 'Your boyfriend?'

Once more the tears flowed, until at last Lisa asked, 'Have you told him?'

'No, and I'm sure if I did he wouldn't want to know.' Sally hesitated for a moment, then she said dismally, 'I think he's gone off me, anyhow. There's another girl he's interested in.'

Lisa stiffened in sudden horrified recognition of a very similar happening—the happening that had changed her own life so drastically. She said quickly, 'First of all you must find out for certain if you really are pregnant, then, if it's confirmed, you'll have to tell him. Why should you bear the burden alone? He's as responsible as you are.' She paused, then went on slowly, 'I once knew someone who was in a similar position, and when she told the man concerned they got married. I believe they're very happy now.'

Sally looked unconvinced. 'Dave wouldn't—he doesn't believe in marriage. Anyhow, I'm beginning to hate him for what he's done to me—he promised——' She broke off abruptly and stared across at the open door. 'Andrew's here,' she whispered. 'He must have come in from the side-door. Do you think he's heard?' She got up quickly and rushed into the dispensary just as Andrew came into the room. He stood for a moment, looking from Lisa to Barbara, then said, 'I'm sorry, but I couldn't help overhearing your—er—discussion.'

'You shouldn't have eavesdropped,' Lisa said sharply. 'Why didn't you cough or something?'

'I'm afraid it didn't occur to me,' he said calmly. 'I was spellbound.'

There was a long silence, then Barbara said, 'I'll just go and see if I can help Sally.' She looked at Andrew. 'I'll pretend you didn't hear anything.'

'Please do. I don't want to embarrass the poor girl,' he said quietly, then he turned to Lisa. 'I was interested in the advice you gave her.'

Lisa looked puzzled. 'Advice? I don't think—oh, well, I just suggested she should tell her boyfriend.'

'She'll be a fool if she doesn't,' he said flatly, 'but then she was a fool to get herself into such a situation in the first place.'

'That's typical of a man,' Lisa's voice was bitter, then, as she saw his eyebrows lift, she added, 'Of course, I don't know the circumstances and I've never met Sally's boyfriend, but from the way she's talked about him, I think he's very demanding and selfish.'

'Yet you suggested she should try to get him to marry her.'

'Oh, stop putting me in the wrong,' Lisa said sharply. 'I merely mentioned a case which had a happy ending.' She paused. 'I was hoping that would persuade her to tell him, but it didn't work. She said —— '

'I heard what she said. She hates him now. So much for love.'

She stared at him. 'How cynical can you get?'

'I have reason to be,' he said, and the bitterness in his voice was reflected in the grim line of his mouth.

'Ah, yes.' She shrugged indifferently. 'The girl you loved and lost to Derek.' She saw him turn pale and pleased to have hurt him, she added coldly, 'Well, that was probably your own fault.'

He stared at her speechlessly and, for a moment, she felt a stab of remorse as, turning on his heel, he strode towards the door. Then he stopped.

'That cat of Olivia's — I must take it round.' Going over to the cage, he picked up a cat basket and opened the door.

'It was sick earlier on,' Lisa said. 'I don't think it was anything more than over-indulgence in mice — temperature normal — but you'd better tell Olivia.'

The next morning was busy, and when an emergency arrived just as they had finished their coffee Lisa began to wonder if it would be possible for her to take her half-day.

A young golden retriever was in a very weak state, and the middle-aged owners were distressed and puzzled.

'We came back from our holiday yesterday and went straight to our friend's house, where we had left Hugo. But she wasn't there, and a neighbour told us she was in hospital with acute appendicitis and Hugo was being looked after by her sister-in-law. When we got to her house we saw at once that something was very wrong with him. The sister-in-law — a disagreeable woman — complained that for the last week he had been vomiting a lot and she was thankful we had come to take him off her hands. We asked her why she hadn't taken him to a vet, but she just shrugged and said the dog wandered and only came back in the evening. We realised then that she had turned him out every day.'

Lisa frowned. 'What a way to treat a dog! Let's get him on the table and see what's wrong with him.' She gazed down at the unhappy animal and said thoughtfully, 'There may well be an obstruction somewhere.'

Her careful examination was followed by an X-ray, and the resultant picture showed that her tentative diagnosis was correct.

'A foreign body in the abdomen,' she announced. 'Look —— ' she held up the X-ray plate ' — it's round — like a small ball.'

'Good God! It could be a golf ball!' Mr Robinson turned to his wife. 'That house is quite near the golf course, and Hugo was allowed to roam about all day.' He paused. 'That means an operation, I suppose.'

'I'm afraid so.' Lisa spoke carefully. 'I don't like doing it as he's so very weak, but there is no alternative.'

Mrs Robinson's voice trembled as she asked the question that Lisa dreaded, and after a few moments' hesitation Lisa said slowly, 'His chances? Honestly I don't know. He's exhausted by this continual vomiting — but he's young, and that is in his favour. I promise you that I'll do my best and we'll watch over him continuously. More than that I can't say. I'll ring you at your home as soon as the operation is over.'

They worked silently — a dedicated trio saving the life of the beautiful dog. The obstruction was, as expected, a golf ball, and once that had been removed without too much difficulty Lisa began to close the wound while Barbara watched over the dog's breathing. It was just as they were about to lift him off the table that his breathing stopped. This was what Lisa had feared, and after a rapid injection of heart stimulant she began giving artificial respiration.

Sally stood back from the table, her hands clasped dramatically over her heart and her eyes wide with dismay. 'I don't think I can bear this,' she gasped, and Lisa glanced up quickly.

'Go away, then,' she said crisply. 'You can't do any good here. Don't faint — go and sit in the office.'

A minute later she looked up at Barbara. 'He's coming back. I think we've done it.'

They worked in silence, and eventually Hugo was lifted carefully and placed in a recovery cage. Heaving a sigh of relief, Lisa turned as Sally came out of the office, looking shamefaced.

'It's no use. I'll never be any good as a veterinary nurse. I hate operations, I feel sick clearing up the mess — all those horrible bits and pieces — washing the instruments, animals being put to sleep. . .' She shook her head sadly. 'It's just not my scene.' She paused. 'I'll have to pack it in.' Then, swallowing hard, she added, 'I'll probably have to anyway if. . .' She stopped and wiped her eyes.

Lisa said quietly, 'I'm sure you're right, Sally; not

everyone is cut out for this kind of work. There's no
need to feel ashamed. You've given it a good try.'

Barbara nodded in agreement. 'You won't follow up
your idea of being a hospital nurse, will you? That
would be even worse.'

Sally shuddered. 'I know,' she said ruefully. 'The
trouble is that I've always had this romantic vision —
ministering angel and all that.' She shrugged. 'Well,
I'm learning fast. Anyhow, I'll stay on until you've
found someone to take my place.' She hesitated, and
once more the tears came. 'I'd probably have to leave
anyway — you know why.'

Lisa nodded sympathetically, then went over to the
recovery cage and studied her patient carefully. Satisfied, she turned to find Barbara standing behind her.
She said, 'I don't really like leaving him. I know it's my
afternoon off, but I think I'll stay on here for a while.'

Barbara heaved a sigh of relief. 'I must say I'm glad,'
she admitted. 'I know I could follow any directions you
gave me — watch out for vomiting, heart stimulant if
necessary — but I'd like you to be near at hand.'

'I tell you what I'll do,' Lisa said. 'I'll stay here for a
couple of hours, then I'll go up to my flat, where you
can get me at a moment's notice.' She frowned. 'Of
course, there's this dinner with James and Angela.
Andrew has to be there too, so you'll have to watch
over Hugo then. He'll have to stay here overnight, but
I'm sure he'll be OK by the evening. Will you ring the
Robinsons and tell them, please?'

Barbara nodded, then added, 'We're really short-
staffed, aren't we? Surely we need another assistant?
And now that Sally. . .' She looked at Lisa curiously.
'Is that what you're going to discuss this evening?'

'Well, obviously something must be done now that
James. . . He's thinking of retiring soon, you know,'
Lisa said evasively. 'Anyway, off you go for a couple of

hours.' She smiled across at Sally, who was reluctantly cleaning the table. 'You, too. I can manage on my own.'

It was good to be alone, and Lisa welcomed the opportunity to concentrate and strengthen herself in preparation for the ordeal that lay ahead. Suddenly she stopped in the middle of tidying up the surgery. Why should it be an ordeal? She was going to be offered a partnership as a reward for work well done in a practice where she was happy, her future was assured—why on earth was she hesitating? The obstacles in her path had all—well, nearly all—been placed there by herself. Admittedly Andrew was to blame for the outbreak of hostilities between the two of them, but she was equally at fault for holding back the information that would put an end to their mutual dislike and constant quarrelling. All the doubts she had felt about the parentage of Jane's child were imaginings which she must keep to herself. It was idiotic to sacrifice her career in order to save Derek and Jane from any possible unpleasantness—trouble that would most probably never arise. All at once she felt as though a great weight had been lifted from her shoulders. She would accept James's offer and, as soon as the opportunity arose, she would tell her story to Andrew.

Filled with elation at her sensible decision, she went to study the condition of her patient, saw that he was making a normal recovery from the anaesthetic, then went to the window to look out on a world that suddenly seemed full of delight. For a few moments she stood there, savouring the relief of having found the right path to follow, when her heart gave a little jump. Andrew's car had pulled into the yard and, as he got out, she saw that his face was drawn and grim. He was frowning when he came into the surgery, and he raised his eyebrows when he saw her standing there.

'What are you doing here?' His voice was flat and tired. 'It's your half-day.'

Quickly she explained the situation, then he said, 'What about lunch? Have you had anything?'

'No, but I'm not hungry. I'll make myself a sandwich later.' Wondering what was the cause of his troubled expression, she tried to speak lightly. 'In any case, I expect this evening I shall be eating far more than I ought. I know from experience that I can't resist Angela's cooking.'

Still frowning, he swept his eyes over her. 'One occasional large meal isn't going to harm you. You're as slim as a needle.'

She laughed ruefully. 'I don't much care for that comparison.'

He shrugged. 'You know very well what I mean.' His eyes surveyed her critically, and she felt her colour rising when he added, 'Looking at you dispassion- ately — as dispassionately as a normal man can when looking at a beautiful woman — I can only say that you are perfection itself.' He smiled grimly at her resentful frown, then suddenly he sat down at the surgery table and passed his hand over his forehead.

'God!' His voice was harsh. 'I'm tired. I've just lost a patient, and that always knocks me up.'

Indignation quickly pushed aside, Lisa was all sym- pathy. This was something she understood only too well. Quickly she produced coffee then sat down opposite him.

'Tell me,' she said softly. 'It might help.'

He looked up at her gratefully. 'Oakhill Farm — a cow in a ditch — been there for hours and hours. She'd strayed away from the herd and was due to calve in a couple of days. The farmer — Mr Bland — should have kept her in, but he's a careless devil — drinks too much and lets things slide. We got her out with great diffi-

culty, because her leg was broken. She was chilled
and shocked—the ditch was full of water—and, in
spite of all I could do, she died. Poor creature. It hurt
me to think how she must have suffered.' He picked up
his coffee and drank deeply, then, just as Lisa was
about to speak, he said, 'I know what you're going to
ask. What about the calf? Well, I did an immediate
Caesarean with the help of Mr Bland, and got out a
nice little heifer. It was a job to get it breathing, but it's
all right now. That was satisfactory, of course, but—'
he shrugged, his eyes bleak '—you know how I feel.'

She nodded compassionately. 'I do,' she said simply.

He gazed at her steadily for a long minute, then he
put his hand over hers and gave a wry smile.

'To lose a domestic pet, well, that's obvious grief,
but a cow—not a very romantic creature—that leaves
most people indifferent.'

'To see any living creature suffer—whether it's lova-
ble or not—causes me pain, as I suppose it does to all
vets,' Lisa said quietly, 'and if I lose a patient it makes
me feel inadequate, makes me doubt my capability as
an animal doctor. It's a horrible grey area and it's very
humbling.' She smiled ruefully. 'It's probably very good
for us and makes us realise that we're not infallible.'

He withdrew his hand in order to pick up his coffee,
and their eyes met as he gazed at her over the rim of
his cup. Lisa felt stunned. This man she thought she
hated had stirred her—touched her heart as no other
man had ever done before. It was a kind of revelation.
No longer poles apart, they were united in a common
cause and united also in their understanding of each
other's feelings. Where those feelings were leading she
dared not hazard a guess, and hastily she tried to lighten
the atmosphere. She smiled self-mockingly.

'Here I am preaching to you as though you hadn't
heard it all before.'

He shook his head. 'You've comforted me,' he said simply.

There was so much warmth in his voice that she flushed deeply, and to hide her embarrassment she got up and went over to inspect her patient. All was normal, and she turned away with a sigh of relief, only to find him still watching her. Nervously she hesitated then said, 'I would really like to go up to my flat — I've got one or two things to do before getting ready for this evening — but I don't like to leave him. Barbara will be coming in later.'

'I'll stay here until she comes — I've had my lunch. Tell me —— ' he put out his hand to stop her retreat ' — have you made up your mind about James's offer?'

Lisa stopped in her tracks. Here was the opportunity she wanted, but it was unkind to disillusion him about the girl he loved when he was in his present state of depression. She nodded.

'Yes. I'm going to accept his partnership offer. It would be stupid not to. That is, if you agree. It seems to me that professionally we can work together quite amicably. As for the personal side, well — we're on different wavelengths there, but I don't think that will affect our work, do you?'

He gazed at her steadily, a strange, unreadable expression in his eyes, and instantly she regretted having posed the question. She turned once more towards the door — better not to wait for his answer — but she was too late. He took a long stride forward, reached for her shoulder, and turned her gently but firmly to face him. She quivered inwardly at his touch and, sensing this, he winced momentarily, but retained his hold on her. She managed to look at him calmly, even indifferently.

Her cool attitude seemed to puzzle him, and his

eyebrows drew together in a frown. When he spoke his voice was strained.

'"Different wavelengths", you say. Undoubtedly, but with a few words of explanation from you we could sort things out.'

For a moment she felt a surge of the old resentment. She gazed back at him steadily. 'I would have given you the explanation the first time we met, but you passed judgement on me without letting me say a word in my defence. If and when I tell you, it will be in my own good time.'

He went very pale and he let her go. 'There is no "if" about it. I'm not prepared to wait much longer. Eventually I shall be obliged to go and see my cousin and get the information from him.' Suddenly his voice softened. 'Lisa, try to see things from my point of view. I feel sure that this is all a storm in a teacup. I know you want to have your revenge, but think of me. I very much want to straighten things out between us.'

The word 'revenge' hit her like a blow. It was so true that she felt humiliated and ashamed. Biting her lip, she stared at him for a long moment, then fled upstairs to her flat. Gazing unseeingly out of the window, she knew that somehow she must put things right. The whole situation was getting out of hand. Revenge was an ugly word, but up till now that *was* what her motive had been. It was contemptible and, in his heart, Andrew must despise her as she now despised herself. She wanted to weep, but with a great effort she held back her tears. Whatever the cost to her pride, she would seize the first good opportunity and be completely frank with him. Then her conscience would be clear.

Gradually her spirits lifted and she began to concentrate on the evening ahead. Angela, she knew, liked people to dress up for her dinner parties, and accordingly Lisa chose her prettiest dress, a soft, clinging hyacinth-blue that matched the colour of her eyes. However it was not for that reason alone that she took such pains with her make-up and arranged her hair in a style that showed it off in all its deep, shining beauty. Subconsciously she knew that she wanted Andrew to see her at her best. The idea confused her, but the feeling persisted right up to the moment when she was welcomed by her host and hostess.

There was, as she expected, a certain amount of reserve in their greeting, but, with the knowledge that her decision would give them pleasure, she felt confident that the somewhat chilly atmosphere would soon disappear.

When Andrew arrived a little later she watched him nervously at first, but he obviously had no intention of spoiling the party by letting James and Angela see that there was any trouble between colleagues. Studying him surreptitiously, Lisa found herself noticing the air of strength and vitality about him, and the laughter in his eyes as he regaled them all with an amusing story about an eccentric client made her realise how very attractive he was. A man, she was forced to admit, to whom in different circumstances, she would have been instinctively drawn. Unconscious that she, too, was being watched, she was startled by a dry observation from her hostess.

'Good-looking, isn't he?' The quiet but pointed remark made her turn quickly, and to her annoyance she felt the colour rising in her face. She managed, however, to nod indifferently and, taking a sip from her glass, she praised the quality of the wine and carefully avoided the other woman's searching and curious gaze.

'I hope——' Angela's voice was still not much more than a whisper '—that you are prepared to discuss matters amicably when we get down to business shortly.

Oh, don't raise your eyebrows like that, Lisa. You know perfectly well what I mean. I don't want James to get agitated.'

Lisa smiled gently. 'Don't worry. I won't upset him. Everything will be OK.'

Angela looked at her doubtfully for a moment, then brightened as Lisa nodded reassuringly. A few minutes later she said, 'We'll have coffee in the other room and relax there while James unfolds his plans for the future of the practice.'

Settled comfortably in an armchair, Lisa waited calmly for the business talk to begin. Glancing at James, she felt a stab of pity for him. How hard it must be to have to give up the work he loved and hand over the practice he had built up so successfully over the years. Absorbed in her concern for him, she was brought back to reality by his repetition of a question.

'Lisa ——' his voice was impatient ' — will you accept my offer or are you still hesitating?'

Quickly pulling herself together, Lisa glanced at Andrew. His face was a mask, showing neither approval nor dissent. Then, as James leaned forward anxiously, she drew a long breath and smiled gratefully at her employer.

'It's a wonderful offer. Generous in the extreme. Of course. . .'

She glanced questioningly at Andrew, and James said sharply, 'Andrew is entirely in favour. Let's be quite open about this. I gather that you and he have your differences — purely personal ones which I gather from him will soon be resolved. So it's entirely up to you, and I hope you will be sensible and not let a golden opportunity be thrown away for some stupid little quarrel.'

Lisa flushed. Put like that, the conflict between Andrew and herself sounded very trivial. James was talking sound commonsense. She drew a long breath and said firmly, 'Thank you, James. It is, as you say, a wonderful opportunity and I would be mad not to take it up. Thank you once again.'

'Ah!' James sighed with relief and sank back in his chair, 'Now you're talking sense at last. Let's all shake hands on it.'

It was when Andrew's hand met hers that she felt the strangest sensation. It was as though her whole life had changed. The future was clearly mapped out and only one thing remained to be done. A firm friendship must be established between her future partner and herself. Still with her hand in his, she realized that he was smiling a little grimly with an unspoken question in his eyes. As James got up to fetch a celebration bottle she said softly, 'He's right, of course. It is a stupid quarrel. Shall we let bygones be bygones?'

He released her hand slowly. 'On one condition, and you know what that is.'

Pushing all past doubts aside, she said lightly, 'No need to look so grim. I promise to tell you what you want to know.'

His expression softened. He lifted his glass and said quietly, 'I'll drink to that.'

After that all tension vanished in the genial atmosphere that now prevailed. Future plans were discussed, James was persuaded to take on the position of consultant, much to his pleasure, and it only remained for the legal side to be arranged. Then, as they stood on the doorstep saying goodbye, Angela bent forward and kissed Lisa, murmuring softly, 'Take my advice and tell Andrew as soon as possible.'

Lisa's feelings were mixed as she drove down the drive with Angela's voice echoing in her mind. Such well-meaning interference irritated her, and it was not until she let herself into her flat that she shook off her resentment. She was being childish once more, she told herself firmly. Angela meant well — everybody meant well, and the sooner she sorted things out with Andrew the better. She must fix a time for a meeting in which they would not be interrupted. A feeling of tiredness threatened to overwhelm her, but determinedly she made a cup of strong coffee and picked up the receiver.

There was surprise mixed with relief in Andrew's voice when he answered. 'That's odd,' he said. 'I was on the point of ringing you. How about dinner with me on Saturday evening?'

'Oh, I don't think so,' she said dubiously. 'I thought maybe we could fix up a meeting in the surgery when Barbara and Sally aren't there.' She paused as a thought struck her. 'In any case, I've got another engagement on Saturday evening.'

'Well, Sunday lunch, then. The King's Arms in Ranford. The restaurant there is very good. I'll book a table and fetch you about midday.'

It wasn't at all what she wanted, but there seemed to be no option, so rather unenthusiatically she agreed, then added hastily, 'No need to fetch me — I'll meet you there.'

Lisa frowned as she put down the receiver, and, remembering David Sinclair, she sighed. Somehow she had lost interest in him and wished she had never accepted his invitation. She had a strong suspicion that she might find him rather boring. Not that she knew very much about him, but he didn't fill her thoughts the way Andrew did.

She frowned again at the realisation that on Sunday she would have to relive hurtful memories, and a wave of dismay swept over her. It was galling to think that she had to give an account of her actions to a man who behaved as though he had a right to know. It was as though she were going to confession in the expectation of receiving absolution when, in reality, she had done nothing wrong. After all, Andrew himself had a bit of explaining to do. Why did he claim that Jane was the woman he loved when he had neglected her to the extent of leaving her to her own devices while he spent several months in Canada? A laggard lover, indeed, if he expected her to wait for his return when there was probably no commitment on his part. As Lisa made her preparations for bed she grew more and more puzzled. There was a mystery there, and if she had to relive her past in order to satisfy Andrew then he, in his turn, ought to confide in her. Comforted by the thought that this put her in a stronger position, she pushed aside all speculation and concentrated on getting to sleep.

CHAPTER FIVE

NEXT morning when Barbara and Sally came into the surgery the latter looked so radiant that it did not need the thumbs-up sign she gave to make it clear that her fears had been unnecessary. She confirmed this when after a fairly quiet surgery they sat down to coffee. She was so jubilant that Barbara said sharply,

'OK, Sally — you escaped this time, so for heaven's sake be more careful in future.'

'Oh, I will be.' Sally nodded solemnly. 'I certainly will. I don't want to go through all that worry again. It's made me realise how untrustworthy men are.' She grinned ruefully. 'I know I was to blame, too, but what I mean is that if I had told Dave that I thought I was pregnant he would most probably just have said, "Tough," and left me to sort things out by myself.' She paused. 'I think I'll take a leaf out of Lisa's book and steer clear of men. Well, for a bit anyway.'

A choked laugh came from behind them and Andrew came forward.

'I couldn't help overhearing that last remark, and I particularly like the last few words.' He shook his head smilingly and went past them on his way to the office. Then he turned. 'I gather your — er — problem is solved. Congratulations!'

As he shut the door behind him, Sally passed a hand over her scarlet face. 'Of all the embarrassing things. He obviously heard me talking the first time I mentioned it. I was afraid he might have, but he ought to have had the tact to keep it to himself. All the same ——' she looked thoughtfully at the closed office door.

'—he's really awfully understanding, isn't he?' She glanced at Lisa. 'I can't think why you two dislike each other so much. Oh, yes,' she said defiantly as Lisa frowned ominously, 'anyone can see that you're like cat and dog together. Of course ——' she paused '—it may be that in reality you're attracted to each other and are subconsciously resisting something so strong that it will eventually——' She stopped as Lisa stiffened and Barbara went off into peals of laughter.

'Look who's talking—the voice of experience!'

Lisa struggled with a strong desire to give Sally a good put-down, then she relaxed and joined in with Barbara's laughter.

'That's all very well,' Sally said indignantly. 'I'm perfectly serious. I think——' She stopped as the office door opened. 'Oh, not again!'

'What's the joke?' Andrew looked at them curiously, then, as they glanced quickly at each other, he added sardonically, 'A purely feminine one, I see. General jubilation at Sally's narrow escape, I suppose.' Then, at the sight of Sally's rapidly disappearing figure as she went to take refuge in the dispensary, he said quietly, 'Let's hope you two can instil a bit of sense into that pretty head and stop her from playing with fire.' He stopped, then shrugged his shoulders. 'In this enlightened age I can never understand why girls get into these scrapes.'

'It's usually because they trust men too much,' said Barbara tartly and went to join Sally in the dispensary, leaving Lisa gazing into her coffee and hoping that Andrew would take the hint and go. To her dismay, however, after looking down at her in silence he asked quietly, 'Do you agree with Barbara? That men are untrustworthy, I mean.'

She shrugged. 'Well, yes. I think they are on the whole.'

He frowned, opened his mouth to retort, but was stopped by the telephone. Forestalling her, he quickly picked up the receiver.

'I think this may be for me,' he said. 'I'm expecting a call from the Ministry about a suspected BSE case.'

He listened for a moment, then with a wry smile he handed her the instrument. 'It's for you. David Sinclair. Your latest conquest.'

Calmly she took the receiver, then waited pointedly till he had left the room. Then she listened to the sound of David's pleasant voice.

'Just to confirm our date for tomorrow evening,' he said, and after a few moments' further conversation she replaced the telephone. But as she stood still for a minute it was Andrew's voice that echoed in her ears.

'Your latest conquest. . .' The mocking little remark annoyed her and, trying to analyse her feelings, she realised that, even now, everything he said seemed to put her on edge. His mere presence made her nervous and shook her self-confidence. Impatiently she thrust her troubled thoughts away and went out to join the nurses in the surgery.

They were discussing the appointments fixed for the next day when the door opened and Olivia Claydon walked in.

'I'm sorry to barge in like this,' she said apologetically, 'but I wondered if you, Lisa, could help me with a small problem.'

Surprised, Lisa ushered her into the office and shut the door. Then she waited, and at last, hesitatingly, Olivia said, 'When Andrew brought my cat back I gathered from something he said that you are very short-staffed here. I thought about it after he left, and it occurred to me that there might be an opportunity for me. What do you think?'

Nonplussed, Lisa stared at her visitor. 'An opportunity? You mean as a trainee nurse?'

'On, no. that's not my thing. I wondered perhaps if you could do with a good receptionist — that's my work in the health centre.'

'But why do you want to change? Surely. . .?' Even as Lisa asked the question she had guessed the answer, and tried not to show her cynical amusement as Olivia said evasively, 'Well, it's the atmosphere here. So friendly — interesting clients. . .' She stopped and shrugged. 'You must know what I mean.'

'Oh, yes,' Lisa said calmly. 'I understand. But it's not up to me, you know. I think you should ask Andrew, though actually I'm not sure that we need a receptionist at all.'

Olivia seemed to have recovered her usual self-confidence as she rose to her feet. She said brightly, 'I certainly will ask Andrew, but what I'm hoping is that you will put in a word for me beforehand, just to prepare the ground.' At the door she turned. 'If you should have any news for me I wonder if you would give me a ring. Then I'll be prepared when I next see Andrew.' She gave a little laugh. 'He's a difficult man to pin down, but I'm hoping to get him to dinner one evening next week.' She paused, gave Lisa a searching look, and added softly, 'David Sinclair is much more approachable, isn't he? I can't quite decide which I prefer. David is taking me out tonight. Should be fun.'

So much for what Andrew called my 'latest conquest', Lisa thought wryly, and, if my instinct tells me right, Olivia was warning me off both Andrew and David. At least until she has decided which one she prefers. Lisa smiled. If only she knew that I don't want either. As for David, he was probably just amusing himself. No doubt he thought there was safety in numbers and, after all, why shouldn't he? A single man

who travelled a lot doing research for his books. . .
Probably it was like the old saying about sailors — a girl
in every port. Lost in her thoughts, she was momentarily startled when the office door opened and Barbara
said urgently,

'Those two cats to be spayed. Have you forgotten?'

'Goodness!' Lisa pulled herself together. 'They completely slipped my mind. Thank you for reminding me.'

Concentrating on each patient as it lay unconscious
on the operating-table, searching with forceps for the
uterus and finally suturing the tiny wound, she found
the time passed quickly, then just as the second patient
was being lifted off the table Sally glanced out of the
window and exclaimed,

'Here comes an emergency — well, it looks it,
anyway. A man getting out of a car with a cat basket —
oh, it's Mr Sinclair.'

She went swiftly to the mirror on the wall and began
to tidy her hair. 'Goodness! I look a wreck!' She turned
away and sighed. 'I wonder what it would be like to be
married to a travel writer. It must be marvellous. All
those romantic places.'

Lisa smiled and Barbara burst out laughing. 'Sally,
do you look at every man with a view to marriage?'

'Only the eligible ones,' Sally said coolly. 'There
aren't many of those around, so I have to keep my eyes
open.' She paused. 'Mr Sinclair is divorced, so he comes
into that category.'

Lisa's eyes widened and Barbara said, 'How on earth
do you know that?'

'I keep my ears open as well as my eyes,' Sally said
calmly. 'Anyway, here he comes.'

It was indeed an emergency. As David placed the cat
on the table he said, 'Blackie has been badly bitten. A
strange cat must have got into the garden. There were
sounds of a feline battle, but by the time I went out to

investigate both cats had disappeared. I've only just found Blackie — hiding in a corner of the gardener's shed.'

Poor Blackie was very cowed and had evidently had the worst of the fight. Examined carefully, he made no protest, and when Lisa looked up she said, 'His ear is badly torn, but I can repair that with a couple of stitches, and there are two rather nasty bites at the back of his head.'

'Oh, dear.' David looked distressed. 'Does that mean a general anaesthetic?'

'I can manage with a local,' said Lisa cheerfully. 'Don't worry, he'll soon be as good as new. I'll also give him an injection of antibiotic as a preventative against the inevitable abscess. Cats are tough, you know.'

'Well, that's comforting.' he smiled with relief. 'May I watch, or will I be in the way?'

Sally cast him a glance that showed quite openly that he would never be in her way, and Lisa, intercepting the look, had to turn away momentarily to hide her amusement. Recovering herself quickly, she said, 'Of course you may watch. It's not the sort of thing that causes people to pass out.'

He laughed. 'I don't pass out easily. I've seen a lot of nasty things in my time.'

Sally cast him another adoring look, but David appeared not to notice anything unusual. He's used to admiring fans, Lisa thought, as she filled a syringe. Waiting for the injection to take effect, she said casually, 'I wonder which cat won the battle. Are there fighters living near you?'

'No.' David looked thoughtful. 'I think Blackie's adversary must be a newcomer to the district. I wonder. . .' He paused. 'Do you think it might be Olivia Claydon's? I saw him the other day when I had

coffee with her. A very tough-looking tom.' He paused
again, glancing quickly at Lisa. 'She got me round there
to sign copies of my books.' He laughed. 'I was surprised to see she had so many — flattered too.'

Bending over Blackie, Lisa suppressed a grin. Full
marks to Olivia! She certainly believed in doing things
thoroughly. It was a good job there was that bookshop
in the nearby village. Then quickly she reproached
herself for indulging in such uncharitable thoughts.
Olivia might well be an ardent reader of travel books.
In any case, there was no reason why she, Lisa, should
begrudge Olivia her friendship with David. He and she
were probably well suited, and their mutual love of cats
would be a common interest. Then, hastily pushing
aside all irrelevant thoughts, she concentrated on her
patient. Quickly and skilfully she repaired his battle
wounds and, the final injection given, she handed him
over to his grateful owner. She said a cool goodbye,
acknowledged casually his reminder of their dinner
date, and tried to ignore the open curiosity in Sally's
face. But it was no use. Sally said half accusingly,

'You never told us you had a date with him. Bang go
all my dreams! Ah, well, you win some — you lose
some. All the same, I wouldn't have said he was the
right man for you, Lisa. Andrew —— '

She stopped as the outer door opened and Andrew
ushered Olivia in. She too was carrying a cat basket
and looked surprised when Lisa laughed and said, 'No
need to tell me. He's been in a fight.'

'Why, yes. How did you guess? Andrew found him
in his garden, and he's got a bite on his front paw.'

'That wasn't the only garden he's been in.' Lisa
smiled. 'He's obviously exploring his new world.'

Olivia looked concerned when she heard about David
Sinclair's Blackie having been treated so badly by her
beloved Spot, and said remorsefully, 'I'll ring him when

I get home and apologise. I hope he wasn't too upset about it.'

Quickly reassuring her, Lisa examined Spot, then, looking up, she said cheerfully, 'Nothing serious. It's as you said — a rather nasty bite on his front paw. I'll soon put that right and give him the necessary injection.'

The job was soon done and Olivia thanked her briefly as she took back the still belligerent Spot, then, turning to Andrew, she said fulsomely, 'You vets are wonderful. It amazes me when I think of the many varieties of animals you have to know about. Lisa here, of course, is very good with small pets, but you — why, you have to deal with so many kinds.' She clasped Spot tightly and shook her head admiringly. 'Cows, horses, pigs and goodness knows what else — so very interesting.'

'Dirty, too.' Andrew laughed, then with a grim little smile he added, 'You mustn't disparage Lisa's work. She is perfectly capable of doing mine as well. And some pretty marvellous operations go on in this surgery, you know.'

Lisa flushed with pleasure at this unexpected praise, and Olivia, quick to sense a rebuke, immediately overwhelmed her with flattery which was so embarrassing that, as soon as she could, Lisa took refuge in the office, leaving Andrew to deal with Olivia. The two nurses went off to the recovery-room, with Barbara vainly trying to stop Sally's barely suppressed giggling. Five minutes later Lisa heard the outer door close and Andrew came in and leant against the wall.

'Phew!' he said expressively. 'That woman is a bit overwhelming, isn't she? I had no idea we vets were so wonderful. Brave in the face of danger, self-sacrificing beings with great hearts full of compassion for the animal kingdom. Heavens! What romantic people we must be.'

Lisa laughed softly. 'Only the male ones. Olivia's

adulation only applied to me when you came so nobly to my defence.'

'Ah!' His mouth twitched at the corner. 'You may well be right.' Then, suddenly serious, he said, 'I don't like women who gush like that. It's so patently insincere.'

Lisa gazed at him curiously. 'You seem to have a very poor opinion of women in general.'

He stared at her sardonically. 'About the same as you have of men, I should think.'

She flushed. 'I'm not fooled by them, if that's what you mean.'

'So we're two of a kind, aren't we? Both disillusioned and both very wary of committing ourselves again.'

Lisa said sharply, 'You're jumping to conclusions again,' then she bit her lip. This was no time to hint at their first quarrel. She added lightly, 'The fact that I'm a bit wary of men doesn't necessarily mean that I'm disillusioned.'

His smile was cynical. 'You could have fooled me.' Then after a moment's silence he said, 'Changing the subject — I hope you'll bear me out when I tell Olivia that I'm too busy to go to her party whenever she brings up the subject again.' He grinned. 'Explain that I'm so dedicated to my veterinary vocation that I shall be spending that particular evening in a cowshed watching over a patient. That's when she has decided on a date. You can tell her at the last minute.'

'I'm afraid you'll have to make that excuse yourself,' Lisa said drily. 'In any case, I shan't be going to the party either, though I haven't yet thought up as unconvincing a reason as yours.'

'Not going?' He stared. 'But one of us will have to go — it would look very discourteous otherwise.'

Lisa's eyebrows rose. 'Is that an order?'

'No. Of course not. How could it be? But surely you will agree that it will look very odd if we both refuse.'

She shrugged. 'Olivia won't mind if I don't go. But you ought to put in an appearance.' She laughed a little mockingly. 'Where's the great hero who is so brave in the face of danger?'

He laughed. 'It depends on the danger. An angry tiger would be preferable.'

'Well, I don't think you have any need to worry,' she said calmly. 'David Sinclair is more in her line. You're probably only a second string to her bow.'

He stared, then frowned. 'Sinclair? But I thought. . .' he hesitated for a moment, 'Don't you mind? I thought you and he —— '

'Oh, for goodness' sake! You seem to misinterpret everything I do or say. Just because I accept a friendly invitation to dinner doesn't mean anything serious.'

'Misinterpret everything?' His mouth set grimly, and her heart sank as he went on, 'Are you referring to what was said at our first meeting?'

She gazed back at him steadily. 'Maybe,' she said, then she went quickly towards the door, but had to stop as the telephone rang.

Picking up the instrument, she listened for a moment then passed it over to Andrew.

'The Ministry of Agriculture,' she said.

A few brief words, then he put back the telephone. Turning to her, he said, 'Would you like to come? I have to meet the Ministry vet at Southlands Farm.'

'Is that the suspected BSE case?' She hesitated, then professional interest took over and she nodded. 'I'd like to — I must admit I've never actually seen one of these cases.'

He frowned. 'That's the worst of doing solely small-animal work. An important part of your veterinary training gets almost forgotten. I think that's wrong. A vet should be able to deal with all animals.'

Shrugging regretfully, she pulled on a jacket and searched for her wellington boots. 'Well, in the case of women, the main reason is that farmers are male chauvinists to a man.'

He took the boots from her as she went to the recovery-room to tell the nurses where to find her, and when she returned he said, 'About the farmers' attitude to women vets—I think they're gradually getting less intolerant. This farm where we're going is one of the more modern ones. Mr Morton always welcomes the women from the Ministry when they come to do the brucellosis test. He treats them with great respect.'

Lisa laughed. '"Great respect"—well, that's a change. Men don't give much respect to women these days.'

He gave her a long look as she got into his car. 'You think it's unusual? In that case I must be unusual, because I have a great respect for women and for you in particular.'

'Oh. That's too much!' Lisa burst out laughing. 'I can't believe that.'

But Andrew didn't join in. Settling himself in the driver's seat, he turned to her.

'But it's true.' His voice was serious. 'I know I've accused you of being devious, but I've come to the conclusion that I've probably misjudged you. I think that if I knew your whole story I would bitterly regret the way I've treated you.'

Lisa's heart was beating madly and she found herself unable to speak. He waited a moment, then with a resigned sigh he turned the ignition key and began to talk of the case they were going to see. He said, 'I'm pretty sure it's BSE. I'm seeing a good many cases these days. However, the experts seem to think they've reached the peak and soon they'll begin to decrease.'

'Of course I've been reading it up,' Lisa said thoughtfully. 'One of the main fears, I believe, is that it may be
transmitted to humans. It's also been found in other
animals — cats and the occasional animal at a zoo. It
seems to me that there is always some connection with
the feeding stuff.'

'That's right, but we can't be absolutely sure.'
Andrew turned down a lane and drove up to a large
farmhouse. Pulling up in the yard, he said, 'No sign of
the Ministry car.'

As they got out, Mr Morton, a tall, burly man, came
towards them, and after a few words of introduction he
said, 'You're a bit early, so would you like to see the
cow? She's no better — worse, in fact. She simply
doesn't know what she's doing. I've isolated her from
the others, of course.'

It was a pathetic sight, and Lisa's heart was wrung
with pity as she watched the black and white Friesian
staggering around in the loose box.

Andrew said, 'No doubt about it now. She's in a kind
of trance, and now, look — she's lashing out at nothing
in particular. Poor creature.' He paused. 'No wonder
they call it "mad cow disease".'

Lisa turned to Mr Morton. 'Is this the first BSE case
you've had?'

He shook his head mournfully. 'It's the third. It's
very worrying, especially as two of the three have
already had calves. I can only hope it hasn't been
passed on to them.'

A few minutes later the Ministry vet arrived, and
after that the unfortunate animal had to be put down.
Then came the grisly task of taking off the head, which
had to be taken back to the Ministry for brain examination. The rest of the carcass had to be burnt as soon as
possible, and, having given all instructions, the Ministry
vet drove away. By that time, Lisa, in spite of all her

training, was looking very pale and feeling rather sick. Glancing at her quickly, Mr Morton said,

'Come in and have a cup of tea. My wife will have it ready. She knows I always get upset at this kind of happening.'

The atmosphere in the farmhouse kitchen was warm and welcoming, and gradually Lisa felt better. Mrs Morton poured out a second cup and said, 'I don't know how you can stand all that, but I suppose you're pretty hardened by now.'

Lisa shook her head ruefully. 'I don't think vets ever get hardened. We have to get used to animals dying or being put to sleep, but, speaking personally, that side of my work is the one I hate.'

Mrs Morton nodded. 'Of course, being a woman makes it doubly hard. At least that's my opinion. Women feel things more deeply than men.'

'Well, that's a nice sexist remark, I must say.' Andrew looked at his hostess quizzically. 'Are you implying that men are hard, uncaring creatures?'

She laughed. 'Well, I'm not sure. Take my Joe here, for instance. When our old collie died he wept like a child and I had to do the comforting. But my sadness was deeper than his, because he now has a new dog which he adores, whereas I find it hard to forget our beloved Larry.'

This started off a discussion which lasted until it was time to leave, and, driving away, Lisa sat in silence for a while. Her thoughts turned back to the sick cow, and at last she said,

'I'm glad I came with you. At last I've seen a BSE case right through.' She smiled wryly. 'That would seem to indicate that I'm hard and uncaring, but I'm sure you know what I mean.'

'Of course I do,' Andrew said warmly. So warmly that she flushed. Glad that he couldn't see her face, she

resumed her silence and found herself acknowledging
that he was utterly different from any man she had ever
met — so different indeed that she hardly dared look
too deeply into her heart to find the reason for the way
in which he affected her.

For the rest of the day she managed to keep out of his
way, but still she could not get him out of her mind. He
was so different from any man she had met. Whether
that was a good thing or not she found it impossible to
decide. It was so difficult to look at him in a detached
way. Perhaps when she had told him what he wanted to
know the war that seemed to be always on the point of
breaking out again would come to an end. Comforted
by the thought, she managed to put him at the back of
her mind for the rest of the day, which passed quietly
until it was time for evening surgery.

It proved to be a very busy one with a great variety
of patients: hamsters, gerbils, pet rabbits brought in by
harassed-looking mothers with children who prowled
restlessly round the waiting room gathering up leaflets
then leaving them on the floor of the surgery; elderly
people torn with anxiety about their beloved com-
panion animals and who, in several cases, had to be
comforted on receiving bad news; recalcitrant, undisci-
plined dogs, and a very large tom cat with blazing eyes
who spat and growled furiously as soon as the lid of his
basket was open. Sally backed away in alarm as his paw
shot out, but when, eventually, Barbara and Lisa
managed to overpower him, his owner became indignant at the force they were obliged to use. Their last
patient was a little Jack Russell who objected so
strongly to being examined that it took the combined
efforts of all three girls to calm him down.

'One would think we were going to murder him,'
Barbara said breathlessly as she handed him over to his

timid-looking owners. 'He's a real little toughie, isn't he?'

They agreed proudly that he was the most difficult dog they had ever had and, as they went out, Lisa laughed ruefully.

'I can't think why people let their pets get the upper hand like that. It must make life very hard for them.'

'They seem to like it,' Sally said. 'Perhaps it gives them the excitement they need, especially if their lives are dull and monotonous.'

Lisa smiled. 'Do you think it's better to live dangerously rather than get into a comfortable rut?'

'It depends on the rut.' Sally grinned mischievously. 'There's one I'd like to be in. It's a dream I have,' she sighed wistfully. 'A wonderful husband who loves me to distraction, a big, untidy house — lots of children, dogs, cats, ponies. . . My idea of heaven.' She stopped, then giggled nervously as she looked towards the door. 'Oh, no! Why does Andrew always appear when I'm saying embarrassing things?'

He stood in the doorway looking amused and, as he came forward, he said with a laugh, 'I'm beginning to think I ought to knock loudly before coming in! I never realised before how much women confided in each other. Their fears, their fantasies — we men seem a dull lot by comparison.' Gazing round the surgery, which had still to be tidied up, he added, 'You appear to have had a pretty hectic surgery. I'm not surprised Sally is pining for the comparative peace of domesticity.' He shook his head thoughtfully. 'You certainly need more help. You can't go on like this. Lisa, come into the office, will you, please? We must sort out this problem.'

Shutting the door behind them, he said, 'Do you think Sally is going to leave?'

Lisa shrugged ruefully. 'She isn't really cut out for

this kind of work, but she say she'll stay until we've found someone else.'

'So not only will we have to get another nurse — hopefully one who is a little less scatter-brained than Sally — but we need another veterinary surgeon. One who can share the small-animal side with you, but who can deal with large animals as well.'

Lisa sighed. 'It's a pity about Sally. I know she's a bit scatter-brained, but I'll be sorry to part with her. She's very amusing — brightens us up no end — and although she says she doesn't like the work, and we all agree that she's not much good at times, somehow lately I've begun to wonder if, in spite of herself, she might succeed after all. Still, there it is. I suppose we'll have to advertise for a replacement. Then as to extra staff — well, there's Olivia. . .' She stopped, biting her lip regretfully. Why on earth, she asked herself angrily, had she let that name slip out so thoughtlessly?

'Olivia? Olivia Claydon? Good lord! What made you think of her?' Andrew stared at Lisa in astonishment, then, seeing her embarrassment, he said slowly, 'Has she approached you for a job here? She already works part-time in the health centre — she must have been joking!'

Lisa drew a long breath before she answered. She said slowly, 'She was quite serious. She asked me to sound you out about it.' She smiled wryly. 'She said she liked the atmosphere of a veterinary practice better than that of the health centre. She would like to be a receptionist here.'

'A receptionist? Well, of course, that's different. I thought you meant a trainee veterinary nurse. Even so —— ' he shrugged doubtfully ' — do you think she'd fit in here?' He added thoughtfully, ' — Do we actually need a receptionist?'

GET 4 BOOKS
A CUDDLY TEDDY
AND A MYSTERY GIFT

Return this card, and we'll send you 4 Mills & Boon Temptations, absolutely FREE! We'll even pay the postage and packing for you!

We're making you this offer to introduce to you the benefits of Mills & Boon Reader Service: FREE home delivery of brand-new Temptation romances, at least a month before they're available in the shops, FREE gifts and a monthly Newsletter packed with offers and information.

Accepting these FREE books places you under no obligation to buy, you may cancel at any time, even after receiving just your free shipment.

Yes, please send me 4 free Mills & Boon Temptations, a cuddly teddy and a mystery gift as explained above. Please also reserve a Reader Service subscription for me. If I decide to subscribe, I shall receive 4 superb new titles every month for just £7.80 postage and packing free. If I decide not to subscribe I shall write to you within 10 days. The free books and gifts will be mine to keep in any case. I understand that I am under no obligation whatsoever. I may cancel or suspend my subscription at any time simply by writing to you.

Ms/Mrs/Miss/Mr _____ 4A4T

Address _____

_____

_____ Postcode _____

Signature _____
I am over 18 years of age.

Get 4 books a cuddly teddy and mystery gift FREE!

SEE BACK OF CARD FOR DETAILS

Mills & Boon Reader Service,
FREEPOST
P.O. Box 236
Croydon
CR9 9EL

Offer expires 31st October 1994. One per household. The right is reserved to refuse an application and change the terms of this offer. Offer applies to U.K. and Eire only. Offer not available for current subscribers to Mills & Boon Temptations. Readers overseas please send for details. Southern Africa write to: IBS Private Bag X3010, Randburg 2125. You may be mailed with offers from other reputable companies as a result of this application.

If you would prefer not to receive such offers, please tick this box. ☐

MAILING PREFERENCE SERVICE

'That's up to you to decide.'

He shook his head firmly. 'We're partners, remember. Any decisions must be mutual.'

Somehow this statement brought home to Lisa the value of her future position in the practice, and she felt a glow that reflected itself in her face and brought a sparkle to her eyes. Impulsively she said, 'It's hard for me to believe. I never expected a partnership so soon.'

He gazed at her in silence, and she flushed under his scrutiny. There was a strange expression in his eyes that she found unreadable. Was it mockery? Or was it dislike at the thought that they would be equals in the practice? Suddenly her elation subsided as doubt swept over her. Involuntarily she said, 'You don't look exactly overjoyed at the prospect. It makes me wonder if our partnership will really work.'

His eyes hardened. 'The only regret I have is that we started off on the wrong foot. Our relations will remain strained until you rectify the situation.'

Angered at his assumption that he was the injured party, Lisa said indignantly, 'That was only because you jumped to conclusions and prejudged me.' Recalling his brutal words at their first meeting, she flared out, 'I shall never forget the things you called me.'

In order to hide the angry tears that were burning at the back of her eyes she turned quickly towards the door, but he reached out swiftly and gripped her shoulder.

'Don't touch me,' she said furiously, but he forced her round to face him and, to her amazement, she saw that he was laughing.

'How lovely you look when you're in a passion,' he said, and, bending his head, he searched for her lips while his eyes grew dark with desire.

Gasping with resentment, she managed to free her

right hand and hit him in the face so hard that he let her go instantly. His breath was coming fast as he put his hand to his cheek, but before he could speak she had whirled out of the room.

CHAPTER SIX

THAT night Lisa's dreams were troubled, a strange mixture of uneasiness and exhilaration. When she woke the uneasiness remained as she remembered the scene with Andrew the previous day. It was a pity that, once again, she had lost her temper with him, and an even greater pity that he had responded so outrageously. Had he really wanted to kiss her or was it just his way of humiliating her? With a sense of shock she found herself wondering what his reaction would have been if she had not attempted to resist. The thought of his mouth pressed on hers made her heart beat so quickly that she jumped quickly out of bed and began to dress, her mind in a turmoil. Drinking her breakfast coffee, she pulled herself together and managed to stifle the strange imaginings caused, she felt sure, by her restless night.

Surgery that morning was cheerful and relaxed, as luckily the patients were only suffering from minor ailments which were dealt with quickly. Remembering that she was going out to dinner with David, Lisa was thankful that there were no serious cases causing problems that might interfere with her engagement. Not that it really mattered very much, but it would be annoying if she had had to put him off yet again. She wanted to get it over, and after that — she smiled wryly — she would leave him to Olivia's tender mercies.

She was in the office when the telephone rang and, leaving it to be answered by the nurses, she gave it no thought. Then Barbara put her head round the door.

'It's Andrew — he wants to speak to you.'

As she picked up the receiver she hoped fervently that there would be no hitch to her plans, but, after listening for a few minutes, her face grew pale. At last she said, 'Of course. Bring the dog in now. I'm free — no operations this morning.'

Her mouth was dry and her heart was thumping madly as she replaced the instrument. Of all the unfortunate things to happen. Andrew's cousin Derek, with Jane, their baby and their dog were on their way to visit Derek's parents, who had retired down on the south coast, and they had called in on Andrew. Apparently their dog, let out for a break on the journey, had become entangled in some barbed wire and was bleeding from tears and cuts on his back. It was, she supposed, the obvious thing for them to get the dog treated before continuing on their journey, but oh, what a trick Fate had played. Why did the accident have to happen at this point in their journey? For a few minutes she gave way to agitation, then gradually she pulled herself together. There was probably no need to worry. Andrew had said he would bring the dog in — he would almost certainly have more tact than to let Derek accompany him, and Jane would no doubt be occupied with the baby. It might even be a good thing in the end. Andrew would see his little relation for the first time and, even if there should be any resemblance to him, it would be put down to a general family likeness. After all, she herself had momentarily mistaken Andrew for Derek when she'd first met him.

Calmer now, she went out to the surgery and saw to her relief, that the nurses were not there. They had probably gone to clean the kennels, and for that she was thankful. Andrew would give her any help she needed with the dog.

Watching from the window, she eventually saw Andrew's car arrive. Then her heart sank. The passenger door opened and Jane emerged, leading a golden labrador, and Lisa drew a long, worried breath. Now their brief acquaintance would have to be acknowledged, and Jane would probably be astonished and dismayed to find that Lisa was working in this practice.

That turned out to be the case, and Jane's face told its own story.

She gave a huge gasp and said breathlessly, 'Lisa Benson! Good heavens!' she turned quickly to Andrew. 'Why didn't you tell me who your small-animal vet was?'

He stared. 'Why on earth. . . I had no idea you two knew each other.' He paused. 'Well—it's a nice coincidence for you, isn't it?'

Lisa, now fully in command of herself, said pleasantly, 'How are you Jane?' She paused. 'And how's Derek?'

'Oh, I'm fine—we're both fine. We have a baby now, you know.' Her voice was nervous and her hand trembled as she pointed to the Labrador. 'Rusty is in trouble, though. He was so restless in the car that we let him out for a run in some fields, but as bad luck would have it he saw a rabbit, went after it and got caught up in barbed wire. We had an awful job getting him free, and you can see he's been cut—there where it's bleeding. We couldn't go on with him in that condition, and luckily Derek remembered that Andrew was living somewhere in this area, so we looked up his address in a telephone book and drove to his house.'

It was a long explanation, and Lisa guessed shrewdly that if she had known who the small-animal vet was she would never have accompanied Andrew to the surgery. The atmosphere was so obviously strained that Andrew looked at them curiously for a minute, then, with a little shrug, he hoisted the dog on to the table.

'It looks as though only a couple of stitches will be needed, but I leave that to you, Lisa.'

After examining the Labrador, she nodded in agreement. 'No other damage,' she said. 'Only needs a local — it won't take long.'

With Andrew holding her patient she worked quickly, and then, as he went into the dispensary to get some antibiotic powder, Jane said in a whisper, 'You haven't told him, have you?'

Lisa stared. 'Told him what?'

'You know what I mean,' Jane snapped. 'Told him the reason why you broke it off with Derek.'

'No, of course I haven't.' Lisa looked puzzled. 'But why shouldn't I?'

'Oh, you mustn't.' She paused. 'You see, as he and Derek are cousins Andrew might let out that I told you I was pregnant. Actually —— ' her green eyes glinted in malicious mockery, ' — I wasn't. I just wanted to get Derek and I thought it was probably the only way to make you give him up.' She stopped, shrugged, and added, 'Oh, you needn't look so scornful. It's all worked out all right — I got pregnant soon after we were married and we're very happy.'

Lisa drew a long breath and stared at her in silence. This girl, devious and selfish, was the one that Andrew loved so deeply that he said his life had been ruined when she married his cousin. It was incredible. Admittedly she was very pretty, with long blonde hair framing a flower-like face. But there was a hard, calculating look in the green eyes that were staring at Lisa so defiantly. Surely Andrew with his keen intelligence ought to have seen how shallow and self-seeking she was. There were many questions she would have liked to ask, but, from the corner of her eye, she saw Andrew coming out of the dispensary. She said lightly,

'It's all in the past as far as I'm concerned. I'm glad you're both happy.'

With a quick, brilliant smile, Jane showed her relief and murmured, 'Silly of me to worry. I thought you might bear me a grudge.'

Taking the antibiotic powder from Andrew, Lisa finished the treatment and stook back as he lifted the dog down from the table. Turning to Jane, she said, 'In ten days' time the stitches must be taken out by your local vet. Rusty is lucky to get off so lightly. Barbed wire can do a lot of damage.'

'I'm very grateful; you've saved me a lot of worry.' Jane turned to Andrew. 'I must get back and see what mischief Jamie has got into. Derek is hopeless—he's too soft with him by far.'

Watching from the window as Andrew's car drove away, Lisa heaved a great sigh of relief. She need have no more doubts about the parentage of Jane's baby, thank goodness. Then suddenly a thought struck her and she frowned. Had she promised Jane to keep her deceitful behaviour secret? She pondered awhile, thinking over their brief conversation. Then, remembering her own evasive answer, she recalled that she had made no such promise. She would, of course bind Andrew to secrecy, but that would probably not even be necessary. He was not the type to want to make mischief between husband and wife. As for his being in love with Jane, if that love still existed, then he was keeping it very well hidden. And Jane, secure in her well-planned marriage, was hardly likely to want to renew any affair they might have had in the past. Perhaps there had not even been any affair in the real meaning of the word. Andrew might only have decided he loved her while he was in Canada and then, meaning to tell her on his return, found himself forestalled by his cousin. It was strange that the dog, Rusty, had been brought in by Jane while

Derek had been left in charge of the baby, but perhaps that had been tactfully managed by Andrew in order to save Lisa the embarrassment of meeting the man she had so nearly married. On the other hand, Andrew might have wanted to be alone with Jane — oh, what was the good of all this surmising? Lisa stepped back from the window and went briskly into the office, where she settled down to paperwork. She worked for an hour, so absorbed in her task that she almost failed to notice that the telephone was ringing. A few moments later Sally opened the door.

'Andrew wants to speak to you,' she said briefly, and as Lisa picked up the receiver she wondered momentarily why it was that her heart always jumped at the sound of his voice.

He said calmly, 'I know you're going out this evening, so I'll do evening surgery. It might be a bit of a rush for you otherwise.'

Lisa's eyes widened. Of course — dinner with David.

'Goodness! I'd completely forgotten. Thank you for reminding me. All the same, there's no need for you to do evening surgery. It won't take me long to get ready.'

'You'd forgotten? Well, I shouldn't tell him that if I were you. It might cool his ardour no end.'

The mockery made her flush and she said sharply, 'Don't be silly. There's no question of ardour on his part or on mine either.'

Irritated, she heard him laugh softly. Then he said, 'I insist. I'll do surgery. Now don't go and forget you've promised to have lunch with me tomorrow.'

He rang off and she replaced the receiver slowly. No, she thought, I certainly haven't forgotten that, and once the atmosphere between us has been cleared I shall probably enjoy it more than having dinner with David.

The thought remained with her as she began to get ready and she wondered wryly how much David really

wanted her company now that he and Olivia were
proving so compatible. He would hardly want to make
another date, and she for her part had no intention of
accepting even if he did. It might be interesting to
sound him out gently on the subject of his friendship
with Olivia. It could help to liven up what promised to
be a rather dull evening.

It was not, however, as dull as she anticipated.
Driving to the restaurant he had selected, he spoke
appreciatively of the countryside, said how much he
liked being based in such a pleasant part of the world,
and compared it favourably with the various countries
in which he travelled in search of material for his books.
Suddenly he glanced across at her and laughed.

'It's all right. No need to be apprehensive. I'm not
going to ask you if you've read them. They're not
everybody's cup of tea. What's more, I'm sure you're
not the type to mug them up in order to feed my vanity.
I've no wish to talk about my books and I'm sure you
don't want me to ask you searching questions about
your veterinary work.' He glanced at her smilingly.
'We're going to dine and wine together and get to know
a little more about each other. I find you very attractive—beautiful, intelligent and. . .well, perhaps I'd
better leave it at that. As for what you think about
me—well, I haven't the slightest idea. Perhaps I'll find
out this evening.'

Lisa laughed. 'Perhaps,' she said and, pondering his
words, she realised that she had given him so little
thought that it was impossible to say whether she liked
him or whether she was utterly indifferent towards him.
In any case, it seemed irrelevant with Olivia in the
background. She and David seemed to have much more
in common and, no doubt, Olivia with her talent for
dealing with men would soon be laying exclusive claim
to him. For some reason Lisa found that idea quite

pleasing. Was it, she wondered, because then Andrew would be in no danger from a woman who would not be at all right for him? But that shouldn't matter one way or the other. Uneasy for a few moments at the direction her thoughts were taking, she told herself that although Andrew meant nothing to her personally it would be very unpleasant to have Olivia in the practice as a partner's wife. Impatiently she shrugged off her troubled thoughts and said apologetically,

'I'm afraid I'm rather dull company. Sometimes it's hard to shake off the day's work.'

David nodded easily. 'That's understandable, but I'm sure a nice meal and good wine will soon put that right.'

The restaurant he had chosen was one that Lisa had heard about but had never visited. Attached to a select country hotel, it was known to be very exclusive. Studying the menu, she gasped a little and said, 'Some of these dishes cost more than we charge for an operation.'

He burst out laughing. 'What a comparison! Talk about being preoccupied with your work. You'll be telling me next that it's cheaper to have a cat spayed than to indulge in lobster.'

'Well. . .' she said dubiously, then, glancing up, she saw the amusement in his eyes and said lightly, 'You're quite right. I'm too wrapped up in my work.'

Relaxed, she made her selection, then, when David had given their order, he sat back and said, 'Now let's talk about each other. I'll begin by asking an important question.' He gazed at her steadily. 'Is there a man in your life who takes precedence over everyone else?'

She blinked, taken aback for a moment, then shook her head.

'No,' she said simply. 'Not at the moment.'

He looked surprised. 'I find that hard to believe. A beautiful girl like you.' He paused. 'Ah, of course. You said "not at the moment", so ——' He picked up his wine glass and studied her thoughtfully over the rim ' — how about letting me fill the vacancy?'

Nonplussed, she hesitated. Then, choosing her words carefully, she said, 'There really isn't a vacancy. I'm not looking for any romantic attachment. I've had enough——' she bit her lip, realising she had said too much, and in an endeavour to cover up her slip she began to praise the quality of the wine.

But it was too late. He said, 'So you've had a bad experience. Well, I won't probe. Instead I'll tell you about myself.' He smiled ruefully. 'Married for five years, no children, then my wife went off with another man. Then divorced. Traumatic for a while, but now I'm fully recovered.' He shrugged. 'One gets over everything eventually. So now I'm looking for an intelligent, attractive woman who will share my life and care for me enough to stay content and faithful.' He grinned suddenly. 'That sounds like one of those advertisements in magazines that come under the heading of "Personal", doesn't it?' Serious again, he asked quietly, 'Do you think I'm asking too much?'

Lisa shook her head slowly. 'No, I don't think you're asking too much.. In fact, you're asking too little. Surely love must come in somewhere?'

He shrugged. 'I'm of the opinion that this love that is so much talked about doesn't really exist. Affection — yes — and kindness — that's important. Mutual interests, sexual compatibility, children — surely that's enough for a happy marriage?'

She latched on to two of his words and said mischievously, '"Mutual interests" — animals. . .cats in particular?'

He nodded calmly. 'Why not? Cats are important in my life. There's something about them appeals strongly to me. They like wandering, exploring, they're very independent but they respond delightfully to their owners.' He laughed. 'Well, I'm not sure if we own them — I think it's probably the other way round.'

Lisa laughed appreciatively. 'A very good description. I'm sure Olivia Claydon would agree with you.'

He stared at her for a moment, then he chuckled.

'Matchmaker! You don't miss much, do you? OK, I'll admit the same idea has crossed my mind, but I've got the impression that she is more interested in your colleague Andrew Morland than in me. However, since you have rejected me so definitely I'll have to give it more thought.' He shrugged ruefully. 'As you will no doubt have gathered by now, there is very little romance in my make-up. I look at things from a totally practical point of view.' He smiled. 'Rather like my cats, in fact. Does that shock you?'

'No,' she said slowly. Why should it? It's probably a very good way of looking at life. I only wish that I ——'

'No, no.' He shook his head firmly. 'You aren't the type. You're an idealist and, in spite of your scientific training, you are at heart a romantic. I only hope your dreams will come true.'

'Oh, dear. You make me sound foolish,' she protested laughingly, but he shook his head once more.

'I envy you and I envy the man who comes up to your expectations. What's more, I have a shrewd idea. . .' He stopped. 'No need to look so startled. I can see you haven't the faintest idea what I'm talking about. Once more I'm looking at things from the practical point of view, but I'm sure I'm right.'

He steadfastly refused to elaborate, saw that she was confused, and adroitly changed the conversation. He was an entertaining host, and the rest of the evening passed pleasantly.

Driving her back, he said, 'Are you going to ask me in for a coffee?'

She hesitated, then, as he pulled up outside her flat, she shook her head. 'No, David, I think not.' She nodded towards a light that showed in the surgery window. 'Andrew seems to have a patient in there. I don't want to give rise to talk.'

'Why not?' he asked lightly, then as he opened the passenger door and let her out of the car he added, 'Someone has just come to the window. I think it must be Andrew. Let's give him something to think about, shall we?'

His kiss lasted so long that she was breathless and indignant. When she managed to break away she said angrily, 'There was no need for that. It may seem amusing to you, but I'm the one who has to live it down. Why did you do it?'

He laughed gently as he got back into his car. Then with his hand on the ignition key he said, 'I thought it might help things along. It's plain to see that you're in love with him — every time his name is mentioned your eyes give you away. As for him — well, a little competition often brings things to a head where a man is concerned.'

Speechlessly she watched as he drove away, then with his astonishing words still echoing in her mind she turned to go up to her flat. Opening the side-door very quietly, she was hoping to slip unobserved up the stairs, but her heart jumped at the sound of Andrew's voice.

'Lisa — would you mind giving me a hand with this accident case, please?' Pointing to a ragged, dirty-looking dog lying unconscious on the table, he added, 'I was on the point of calling out one of the nurses when I heard David's car pull up outside.' He gave her a twisted smile. 'I hope you won't mind coming down to earth after what must have been a romantic evening. All right! No need to glare at me, here. . .' He took her overall down from its peg and held it out. 'Mustn't mess up that beautiful dress.'

She snatched it from him, flushing hotly. 'And there's no need for you to be sarcastic. It was not a romantic evening. It was——' She stopped abruptly. It was nothing to do with him anyway. Drawing a long breath, she went up to the table and, after gazing at the unfortunate dog she said, 'He looks very bad. What happened to him?'

'I found him in the road. Hit by a car, I imagine. I think he's had it—probably bleeding internally. I've tried all the usual things. I'm now going to give a blood transfusion although. . .' He shrugged grimly. 'Well, must try everything.'

She nodded and, while they were working together, the tension between them disappeared as concern for their patient took over. All to no avail, however, and when at last Andrew lifted the dog down from the table he said, 'I'll ring the police in the morning.'

Lisa looked at her watch. 'It's morning already.'

'Good lord!' Suddenly he put his hand on her shoulder. 'I shouldn't have dragged you into helping me with what was almost certainly a hopeless case, but you know how it is—one always hopes to win the fight.' He sighed. 'Well, in this case it was probably all for the best—a poor, thin, neglected animal. Thank you for all your help. You must be very tired.'

She nodded and as she fumbled with the buttons of her overall he said, 'Let me help you, now.' Taking it from her, he stood looking at her with a strange expression in his eyes. Surely, she thought, he couldn't have guessed at the odd sensation she felt at the touch of his hand.

She turned away as suddenly David's farewell words rushed into her mind, and in an effort to dismiss them she said hurriedly, 'You look tired too. Shall I make a coffee?'

He hesitated, then in a voice that sounded strained, he said, 'No, thanks. I don't think that would be very wise. I'll clear up here and lock up. You go and get your beauty sleep.' His eyes swept over her. 'Not that you look as though you need it.' Then, half mockingly, he added, 'You must have had a very — er — pleasant evening out. You're still all aglow.'

Her colour faded as she stared at him. How could she possibly explain the reason for David's apparently ardent kiss? She stood silent, then, as though echoing her thoughts, Andrew said, 'There's no need to look so embarrassed. It's none of my business.' He held the door open for her. 'Goodnight, and all my thanks. See you tomorrow for lunch.'

It all meant another restless night for Lisa. David's assumption that she was in love with Andrew both irritated and worried her. Recalling Andrew's tenderness and compassion when dealing with his patients, she acknowledged that it was only natural that that side of his character should appeal to her, but there was no question of her being in love with him. It was just a figment of David's imagination. The fact that her heart always beat faster at the touch of Andrew's hand troubled her a little, but with a shrug she dismissed the thought. It was, after all, the normal reaction of any woman to an attractive man. Nevertheless she still felt uneasy, and her apprehension grew as she remembered that she was lunching with him the next day. At last she drifted off to sleep and dreamt that she was running wildly away from something that threatened to overtake and overwhelm her.

In the morning her spirits lifted. Brilliant sunshine filled her room, and the trees outside stood golden and glowing under a sapphire-blue sky. Filled with energy, she cleaned her flat, then after a quick shower she stood surveying her range of clothes. Autumn colours were definitely called for, and when she had made her selection she smiled with satisfaction. Taking a last look at herself in the long mirror, she wondered fleetingly why she had taken so much trouble over her appearance. Then she shrugged indifferently. Of course it was merely to give herself confidence — confidence that she was going to need badly in the ordeal that lay ahead.

Nevertheless when she saw the appreciative look in his eyes she flushed involutarily as she got into his car. He himself was wearing well-cut casual clothes and looked so handsome that in spite of herself, her heart gave a little leap of excitement. But his first words were unwelcome.

'So what was it like — your evening with David Sinclair?'

Fixing her eyes on the road ahead, she hesitated before answering, then said lightly, 'Very nice. A wonderful meal and interesting talk.'

'Ending on a highly romantic note.' His voice was dry, then he added quickly, 'Sorry. I've no right to pry. I don't want to annoy you. We mustn't start quarrelling again.'

'It's difficult not to,' she said sharply. 'We always rub each other up the wrong way, don't we?'

He shot her a quick glance. 'We must try to find a cure for that. I, for one, don't like the cat-and-dog atmosphere that exists between us.' He paused for a moment, then gave a short laugh. 'Talking of cats, Olivia Claydon rang me yesterday evening to ask if I knew where she could get hold of a well-bred kitten. She thinks it might stop her present one from wandering.'

Lisa raised her eyebrows sceptically. 'I should have thought she could find one for herself.'

'Yes, I thought the same. However. . .' His mouth twitched at the corner and he left the phrase unfinished.

'Well, it made a good excuse for ringing you up,' Lisa said caustically, and bit her lip as he laughed aloud.

'How well you women understand each other. That was a bit catty, though, wasn't it?'

Lisa frowned. 'I don't really understand Olivia. I know nothing of her past, so I shouldn't have said that. I expect you know her better than I do.'

'Perhaps I do,' he said slowly. 'I believe she's had rather an unhappy time. Her husband was unfaithful and made no secret of it, and now that they've broken up she's rather at a loose end. I sympathise with her, but that's all. As for this idea of working with us—I don't care for that much. She's fond of animals, of course, but that doesn't really mean a thing. Would you like to have her in the practice? You'd be more affected by her presence than I would.'

'I don't think she'd fit in very well.' Lisa hesitated. 'What's more, she wouldn't stay long. She's out to. . .' she stopped, then added lamely, 'Well, she might get married again. Not, of course, that that would stop her working if she wanted to, but. . .' She shrugged. 'I'll leave the decision to you. If you want her in with us I'll accept her.'

Andrew nodded but said nothing, and there was silence until at last, he slowed down the car. 'Here we are,' he said. 'The King's Arms. Let's hope I can find a place to park. It looks very full.'

When eventually they were seated at the table he had booked Lisa suddenly felt depressed. This was the time she had chosen to tell him what he wanted to know, but she loathed the idea of reliving all the trauma of things long past. She certainly wouldn't bring up the subject until he did. Suddenly she started as his voice broke into her thoughts.

'It's an interesting menu. Have you made your choice?'

Hurriedly she pulled herself together and made her selection, but her appetite had flagged and it was not until she had drunk a little wine that she began to revive.

'That's better,' he said approvingly. 'I was beginning to wonder what was wrong. You seemed rather distant.' He laughed. 'Or shall I say more distant than usual?'

She flushed. 'I'm not distant — I'm just nervous.'

He gazed at her steadily. 'Nervous? Oh, I see what you mean. Look, Lisa, I've been thinking. I'm not going to press you to tell me anything you don't want to. I'm sorry I behaved the way I did. You told me that you broke off your marriage plans because you found you didn't really love Derek — that much I know — and I realise now that you did the right thing. Seeing Jane yesterday made me understand how one can be mistaken about love.'

There was a long silence, and now Lisa was consumed by curiosity. She longed to know more, but Andrew evidently felt that the subject was closed. Distracted, she found it difficult to concentrate as he began to talk of other things, and when he stopped in the middle of a sentence she was still absorbed in her thoughts and took no notice. At last he said quietly, 'I'm sorry. I'm obviously boring you.'

Shaken by her lack of courtesy, Lisa flushed vividly.

'No — no — of course I'm not bored. It's just that. . . well, I'd like to ask you some questions, but they're personal and I'm afraid you will resent them.'

He said calmly, 'Try me.'

Drawing a long breath, she plunged in recklessly. 'Did you have an affair with Jane before you went to Canada?'

His eyebrows went up and immediately she said

hurriedly, 'I'm sorry. I take that question back. I shouldn't have asked you — it's too personal.'

'OK,' he said evenly, 'we'll cut that one out. So — pass on to the next.'

Wishing she had never brought up the subject, Lisa went on. 'Why did you stay so long in Canada if you were so madly in love with her?' She paused, noticing that his eyes had grown hard, and added, 'Look, if you think I'm being too intrusive don't bother to answer that question either. Forget the whole thing. Let's talk about something else.'

He shook his head. 'You've asked me, so I'll tell you. I went to Canada in the first place as a kind of escape. My parents were recently dead and I thought perhaps that a new life in a different country might help to heal the wound. I had a vague idea that I might settle there. A friend of mine — a fellow vet — had a good practice just outside Toronto, and I was tempted to join him. After a while I realised that I didn't like it all that much and, thinking of all I had left behind, I found myself longing to get back — and longing to see Jane again. I was half in love with her when I left England, and as I concentrated on her I felt that that love had grown into the real thing. So I determined to leave Canada — she would have hated it anyhow — and ask her to marry me.' Andrew's mouth twisted suddenly. 'Of course I was shattered when I found I was too late.' He took up his glass, drank some wine, then added slowly, 'I was furious with myself for not having told her of my love — I really. . .well, I literally went through hell.' Suddenly he pushed his plate aside and leaned back in his chair. Then he said harshly, 'I know now that I was a damn fool. I had built up a dream girl who didn't exist, and I was still deceiving myself when I met you — the girl who was the cause of all my disappointment.'

'The cause of — oh, now that's most unfair,' Lisa said indignantly. 'How can you think that?'

He twisted the stem of his glass. 'Well, if you hadn't chucked my cousin he wouldn't have turned to Jane and married her — probably on the rebound from you.' He shrugged. 'That was how I reasoned it out, but you're quite right. I shouldn't have blamed you. You couldn't have known what was going to happen.'

Throwing caution to the wind, Lisa burst out impulsively, 'But I did know. I had a visit from Jane, and it was because of what she told me that I gave Derek up.'

He stared at her incredulously. 'What did she tell you?'

She shook her head slowly. 'I don't think I want to go into that.'

For a few moments he sat deep in thought, then, looking up, he smiled cynically. 'I can guess. I wasn't born yesterday. It's the old, old story. She'd been having an affair with him and was pregnant.'

'That was what she told me, and she said Derek was the father. Naturally I believed her. She gave me chapter and verse of the times they had been together. It was only afterwards, long afterwards, when you spoke of your love for her that I began to wonder if perhaps the child was yours, and Jane, thinking you had deserted her, had decided to marry Derek.'

'You thought that? Thought that I. . .? Good God! I'm not the child's father — I didn't have an affair with her. It never got as far as that.'

'Well,' Lisa said slowly, 'it worried me a lot, and it was only when Jane told me yesterday that she had pretended to be pregnant in order to get Derek that I knew how I had been deceived.' She stopped. He was staring at her so intently that she grew nervous. At last she said, 'Please don't stare at me like that. Don't you believe me?'

'Of course I believe you. What surprises me is that you show no bitterness. A vile trick played on you like that — your life ruined. . . That's how it must have seemed to you at the time.'

She gave a wry smile. 'I got over it. Especially when I began to realise that I wasn't really in love with Derek. In a way I was grateful to Jane for having saved me from an unhappy marriage.' She paused, lowering her eyes in order that he should not see the tears that were threatening to fall. 'It was your accusations that really hurt me. You said I was hard, selfish, callous — '

'Don't. . .' He leant forward and took her hand. 'I'll never forgive myself. I just hope *you* can forgive me. Is that hoping too much?'

She blinked hard and looked up. 'It was all a dreadful misunderstanding. Of course I forgive you.' She tried to withdraw her hand, but he retained it for a minute longer. Then, as he released it, he gazed at her so penetratingly that she felt her colour rising. Embarrassed, she said, half laughingly, 'You're staring at me as though I'm something under a microscope.'

He smiled. 'What a picture you conjure up.' Leaning back in his chair, he said slowly, 'The reason I'm staring at you is that I'm seeing you properly for the first time.' Picking up his glass, he added, 'Let's drink to our future together as friends and partners.'

CHAPTER SEVEN

THE silence between Andrew and Lisa as they drove back was not oppressive. Rather it seemed that with the ending of tension between them they each felt such relief that speech was unnecessary. Then suddenly, with a muttered exclamation, Andrew pulled up abruptly.

'Look — look — over there.' He pointed over to the right. 'Those dogs — two of them — they're chasing sheep!'

He was out of the car and pulling on his boots almost before Lisa had grasped the situation, and had climbed the gate and was well ahead as she endeavoured to catch up with him. He shouted as he ran, and the dogs — a large Alsatian and a black and white mongrel — hesitated for a moment, then, in the throes of killer lust, continued their chase. Two of their victims were lying ominously still behind them, and a group of terrified sheep huddled up in the far corner of the field began to scatter in panic. Then at the sounds of fury behind them the dogs hesitated once more, turned and, seeing the two figures waving and shouting in anger, took fright. Abandoning their quarry, they made off, pushing their way through the hedge at the far side of the field.

Gasping for breath, Lisa caught up with Andrew as he bent over the first of the two ewes lying on the ground. He looked up, his face grim.

'Nothing to be done about this one. Badly bitten and dead from shock. Let's have a look at that one over there.'

There was blood on the other ewe's back, but she

118

was still alive and endeavoured to rise to her feet as
they approached. Then, managing to stand for a
moment, she gave up and collapsed once more on to
the grass.

'We'll have to get her back to the farmhouse somehow. It's over there.' Lisa pointed, and Andrew
nodded.

'An injection first, though,' he said. 'My case is in
the car. Would you. . .?' Glancing down at Lisa's feet,
he said, 'No, I'll fetch it. Your shoes — what a state
they're in! You shouldn't have come. Well, stay here
with her — I shan't be a minute.'

Gazing down at her ruined shoes, she shrugged
ruefully, then, bending down, she tried to calm the
injured ewe. The blood, she saw, came from a large
gash across the animal's back, but as far as she could
see there were no other injuries. It was with a sigh of
relief that she welcomed Andrew back and watched as
he opened his case and filled a syringe.

'I was lucky,' he said breathlessly. 'There was a
tractor working just over the hill, so I've told the driver
and he has gone to contact Mr Marsden, the farmer.
They'll be along soon with a pick-up truck.' He withdrew the needle. 'That should help to deal with shock.
I'll stitch her up if she survives until we get her back.'
Gazing around, he added, 'That hole in the hedge
where the dogs went through — Mr Marsden will have
to get that mended at once. He really should have
barbed wire as well.'

A few minutes later the pick-up truck arrived and
drove across the field, and as the farmer got out Lisa
saw that his face was flushed in anger, while the farm
worker beside him looked as though he had had a
strong dressing-down.

'Blasted dogs,' he said furiously. 'They're the plague
of my life. There's a new estate in the village, and the

people who live there have mostly come from the town. They seem to think that because there are fields round them they can turn their dogs out and let them roam everywhere. Mind you——' he turned to glare at his unfortunate farm worker '—if you hadn't been so careless they wouldn't have been able to get in. You'll have to work overtime to get that hedge repaired and wired up.' He paused and looked at Andrew. 'Can't thank you enough,' he said gruffly. 'I believe you told the tractor driver that you're a vet. Well, my old vet has sold his practice and I don't like the young fellow who's taken his place.' He shrugged disgustedly. 'I don't think he's been qualified long. Doesn't seem to know much about farm animals, so will you take on my work?'

Andrew looked nonplussed. 'Well, it's a question of etiquette—but we'll have to go into that later. Meantime, this ewe. . .'

'Ah, yes.' Mr Marsden looked down and shook his head despondently. 'Best get her into the truck. Will you be able to treat her straight away or will you have to get anything from your surgery?'

Andrew held up his case. 'I've got everything necessary here and——' he nodded towards towards Lisa '—another vet to help me.' He paused. 'My partner, Miss Benson.'

The farmer looked up as he and his man were about to lift the ewe into the truck. 'Well, I'll be. . .' He stared at Lisa, then gave her a slow grin. 'Two for the price of one, I hope. Not going to charge me double, are you?'

Andrew shook his head and grinned. 'You farmers!' Then he added, 'We'll discuss all that later. But first of all we must get this poor creature seen to. Then you'll have to inform your present veterinary surgeon that you no longer require his services. When that's all fixed up, I'll gladly do your work.'

Watching the pick-up truck bumping slowly back over the field, Andrew said apologetically, 'Sorry about your shoes, Lisa. You'd better charge another pair up to expenses.'

She smiled wryly. 'That's taking things a bit far, but we certainly lead a strange life. All the same, I wouldn't change it for any other work.' He paused and glanced at her curiously as she picked her way carefully over the field. 'Would you want to continue practising if you got married?'

Startled at the direct question, Lisa hesitated. At last she said slowly, 'I'd hate to have to give it up. Come to think of it, I remember that when I was engaged to Derek the question did arise, and he wasn't at all keen on the idea. But I was firmly resolved to continue as a vet, even if it meant running a small clinic from our home. He had to agree in the end.'

'I expect he thought the price was worth paying,' Andrew said drily. Then, as he shut the field gate behind them, he added, 'Well, he hasn't got that particular problem with Jane.'

Wondering what was behind that remark, she said nothing, but after they had settled themselves in his car he turned to look at her.

'In answer to your unspoken question — no. I have no more regrets. I was completely mistaken in Jane.' Astonished at the way in which he had read her thoughts, Lisa remained silent, and as he turned the ignition key he went on thoughtfully, 'Infatuation can so often be mistaken for love.' He shrugged. 'Sometimes, though, I wonder if there is such a thing. Real love, I mean. Jane and Derek seem reasonably happy, though I don't suppose there was anything more between them at first than a desire to get married.' He slowed down to negotiate a sharp turning in the lane, then he said softly, almost as though talking to himself, 'That's not enough for me. I want a love that burns me up and is so deep and strong that it will last a lifetime. I suppose everyone wants that, but I don't think it happens to many, if it exists at all.' Suddenly he glanced sideways at Lisa. 'Do you have the same dream, or would you settle for compatibility?'

'Oh, no!' She shook her head emphatically. 'I'd rather stay single for the rest of my life.'

'Hmm! I don't see that happening to you.'

There was a hint of mockery in his voice, but there was no opportunity to reply, because they were now going up the drive to the farmhouse.

On arrival Mr Marsden led them across the yard to a loose box and said, 'Well, if you don't need me I'll go and ask my wife to get tea for you. Come in when you've finished.'

The ewe was docile and easy to control, and Andrew and Lisa managed to do a successful job in spite of the rather primitive conditions. It was with a feeling of satisfaction that they entered the farmhouse kitchen and Andrew said, 'I think she'll be OK now, but she'll need watching for a while. She's been very badly shocked.'

Mr Marsden nodded gratefully. 'I'm thankful you came along when you did. God knows how many sheep those damned dogs would have killed if they'd been left to it.' He sighed heavily. 'Farming is difficult enough nowadays without dogs hunting like wolves. If I ever manage to catch them at it again, I'll shoot them, and I'll be fully entitled to. Then all the do-gooders will accuse me of brutality, I suppose.' He shrugged. 'Well, there it is—farmers are always in the wrong. We're always being told what we must do, what we must grow in the way of crops and lord knows what else by a lot of city slickers who don't know a bullock from a bull.' He pulled out a chair for Lisa. 'Now come along, miss, sit you down and sample my wife's scones. I reckon she's the best cook in the county.'

It was an enjoyable tea, although Lisa found it difficult to do it justice, coming as it did so soon after the lunch she had had with Andrew. She had just refused a second slice of cake when Mrs Marsden got up, filled a saucer full of milk, and said,

'Our cat has just had another litter. Sweet little kittens, but the difficulty is finding homes for them. One was born dead, but that still leaves five. Come and have a look at them. Perhaps you could put a notice up in your surgery.'

Following her out to a large, warm scullery, they saw the mother cat lying in a large box with her kittens curled up round her. Mrs Marsden picked them up one by one and, after examining them, Andrew turned to Lisa.

'What do you think? Shall we tell Olivia?'

Lisa nodded. It seemed the obvious thing to do. She said, 'She'll have to wait till they're weaned.'

'Well, I'll bring her over here,' Andrew said, 'then she can make her choice and fetch it when it's old enough to leave its mother.'

Sitting beside Andrew as he drove back, Lisa felt unaccountably depressed. Trying to analyse her feelings, she was forced to admit that her uneasiness was caused by the thought of Olivia and Andrew together. Startled at the realisation, she tried to push it aside, but without success. Impulsively she said,

'Why don't you save yourself the trouble and just give her the address? She might get David Sinclair to go with her—they're both so fond of cats. He might even take one himself.'

For a moment Andrew seemed to consider her suggestion. Then he shook his head. 'No, I'd better go with her. She'll want my advice. In any case, I shall have to call here again in ten days' time to take the stitches out from the ewe.'

Faced with the inevitable, Lisa said no more, and it was not until Andrew pulled up outside her flat that she said, 'It would be silly to ask you if you'd like some tea after that enormous spread at the farm, but would you like to come in for an early drink?'

He looked pleased, and a few minutes later as he sank into an armchair in her sitting-room he said, 'By the way, I forgot to tell you over lunch. Remember your idea for a part-time veterinary assistant? Well, I think I've found one. Name of Roger Ballard. I met him in Canada and he's over here now, searching, he says, for the ideal job.' He laughed. 'I told him there was no such thing—he rang me yesterday, asking me if I knew of anything that would appeal to him. Well, I asked him if he'd like a part-time job here, and he jumped at my offer. Of course it depends on what you think of him. Would you like me to give him a ring and fix an appointment?'

She nodded and watched as he went over to the telephone. Seeing him here in her flat was doing strange things to her heart. His presence seemed to fill the room. His tall figure, deep voice, the whole masculinity of him was unnerving. From being adversaries, they were now friendly colleagues, and that should satisfy her, but deep inside something was stirring—something vaguely unsettling. It was a feeling she hardly dared to analyse. Uneasily she got up and stood beside him as he talked. Casually he reached out and put an arm across her shoulder and, half turning, he nodded and smiled. Then again he spoke into the receiver.

'Good. So how about coming over to my house this

evening? We'll discuss it over a drink. About eight—yes.'

Replacing the instrument, he asked, 'Is that OK?'

She nodded her assent, slightly bemused at the speed with which he had put her idea into practice. Very conscious of the pressure of his arm, she withdrew gently and, just as casually, he took it away. It meant nothing, she told herself. It was just a friendly gesture to draw her into the conversation. They had barely had time to sit down when the telephone sounded again. This time she picked up the receiver and heard Olivia's voice.

'Lisa—I've been trying to get Andrew. Do you know where he is?'

Putting her hand over the receiver, she turned to Andrew. 'It's Olivia. She wants to speak to you.'

He shrugged ruefully and, taking the instrument from her, he said, 'Hello, Olivia. What can I do for you?' He paused and listened, then he said, 'Yes. I'm in Lisa's flat. Now what's the trouble?'

When next he spoke his voice was cool. 'Well, why don't you try David Sinclair? Your cat has probably gone over there again.' Then with a little more warmth he added, 'By the way, I think I've found a kitten for you, but I'll tell you more another time.'

He stood for a moment before returning to his seat, then, turning, he met Lisa's raised eyebrows. He grinned. 'You don't need to say it. She didn't like my being here in your flat. I expect she thinks we're up to no good.'

Lisa laughed but said nothing. Why was it, she wondered, that he didn't seem to mind Olivia's possessive attitude? Was it because he was too indifferent to care, or was it because he was secretly rather flattered? Certainly he seemed keen to take her over to see the kittens. She frowned slightly, then noticed that Andrew was looking at her searchingly.

'What's wrong? Don't you like the idea that Olivia knows I'm here with you? It's nothing to do with her, surely?'

'Of course it isn't, and it doesn't matter to me in the least.' Quickly she turned the conversation and, after a moment's hesitation, he followed her lead. But the atmosphere was stiff, and it was not until Andrew got up to leave that he seemed to relax.

'I'd better be going. You won't forget this evening at my house, will you?'

'I'll be there,' she promised and smiled.

Looking at her steadily for a few moments, he asked quietly, 'Everything is OK now, isn't it? We're friends from now on, aren't we?'

She nodded again and, bending forward, he kissed her gently, then with a quick goodbye he was gone.

For a few minutes she sat quietly, trying to sort herself out. Perhaps it was because she had not yet accustomed herself to this new relationship that she was so ill at ease with him. It was just a question of adjustment on her part. Andrew seemed to have no difficulty, so why should she? The question remained unanswered, but resolutely she thrust it into the back of her mind. She was getting too introspective, she told herself, imagining problems where there was none.

It was chilly at eight o'clock that evening, and on arrival at Andrew's house Lisa welcomed the log fire burning brightly in the room into which she was ushered. A tall man stood up as she entered, and while Andrew made the introductions she studied the stranger carefully. He was in his late twenties, with brown hair, and brown eyes in a craggy sort of face. She subconciously registered him as a gentle giant. He seemed rather shy, flushing a little and stammering slightly as he answered her polite questions about veterinary life in Canada.

There was a small cynical smile on Andrew's face as he observed the effect Lisa was having on his friend. Handing round drinks, he said, 'Lisa works wonders in the small-animal side of this practice, and as a result of her popularity with clients she is in danger of getting overworked. The evening surgeries in particular tend to go on far too long, and that's where your help would be most needed. Then you could fill in on our days' off — do a bit of weekend duty et cetera.' He paused. 'It sounds a bit vague, but you know how erratic veterinary work is. Would you like to come and help us out in this way?'

With his eyes on Lisa, Roger said, 'It would suit me very well. You seem to have a flourishing practice with plenty of scope for future development.' He turned to Andrew. 'If all goes well and you find my work satisfactory, would you consider taking me on eventually as a full-time assistant? As you know, I really want to settle in England. My parents went to Canada when I was a boy, and I've always had this kind of homesickness for the country in which I was born.'

Andrew glanced quickly at Lisa, then he said, 'Well, I did think of suggesting that, but, if you remember, you told me you only wanted to work part-time.'

Roger laughed a little self-consciously. 'That's what I've been doing up till now, but I've got this kind of gut feeling that at last I've found the ideal practice in an ideal part of the country.'

Andrew's eyebrows rose quizzically for a moment, then, turning to Lisa, he asked, 'What do you think? Shall we consider this part-time work as a kind of trial period? Give it, say, a month, then discuss the future?'

She nodded. 'It's a good idea. As for the evening

surgeries, we could extend their length and divide the time between us.'

Andrew said slowly, 'If we do that, then Roger could take the latter half and also do any calls that come in for you during the evening and night.' He turned to Roger. 'I don't like Lisa doing outside calls at night on her own. Even if the call comes from a client she knows, I still think she should be accompanied.'

Lisa stiffened and began to remonstrate, but Roger forestalled her. 'I absolutely agree with that. You sure can't be too careful these days.'

Lisa said scornfully, 'I've never had any trouble during the time I've been here. I'm not a fool—I generally insist that unknown clients should bring their pets to the surgery.'

'Hmm! What about David Sinclair? You didn't know him from Adam, yet you went dashing out when he told you he'd rescued a dog he found in a ditch. As it happened, it was a perfectly genuine case, but it could easily have been. . .' He shrugged. 'Well, use your imagination.'

Lisa flushed, drew a long, angry breath, then subsided. This was not the time to get into an argument. She shrugged evasively and said nothing, while Andrew went on to discuss accommodation.

'We haven't a flat available at the moment, but I've got plenty of room in my house and a good housekeeper who comes in every day, so you can move in when you like.'

'Perfect.' Roger's pleasure was evident. 'I'll go and pack up my things right now.'

When he had gone Lisa said thoughtfully, 'I wonder why he decided so quickly that this was the perfect practice for him.'

'Surely you guessed?' Andrew grinned. 'He was hooked from the moment he saw you.'

'That's ridiculous!' Lisa said scornfully. 'No man in his senses would decide his future for such a flimsy reason.'

'I do believe, Lisa —— ' Andrew was suddenly serious '— that you have no idea of the effect you have on men.' He studied her with a penetrating gaze which she found rather unnerving. She said hurriedly, 'I must go. Lots of things to do.'

'Don't go yet. Have a coffee with me.' His attitude was so friendly that she felt it would be churlish to refuse. In any case, she really wanted to stay. There was something about him that fascinated her and made her want to get to know him better. While he was in the kitchen she wandered round the room, admiring the pictures, and examining the books which took up the whole of one wall. One shelf was filled with veterinary subjects, but the ones that interested her most were those that filled the other shelves. They were so varied and, in several cases, they reflected her own tastes. His collection of books on serious music was surprising, and she was absorbed in a study of the works of Schubert when Andrew came back and placed a tray on a side-table.

'Are you interested?' He indicated the book, and when she nodded he added, 'Let's have some Schubert, then. What would you like?'

She said promptly,'The "Unfinished" Symphony. I love it. It's so mysterious. . .seems to come from another world.'

As the lovely sounds filled the room, she drew a long breath of pleasure. It was all so perfect, this being at one with Andrew. Absorbed in the music, they sat in easy silence until, as the majestic chords of the first movement came to an end, Andrew said quietly, 'Music like this is food and drink to me. It puts everything into perspective.'

She nodded, but said nothing. He was right, she reflected; all the niggling problems and worries of the day seemed trivial, and were washed away on a tide of glorious sound. Once more they sat silent as the second and last movement with its lovely melody held them enthralled, and when at last it came to an end Lisa sighed regretfully. She said, 'I always wonder what the third movement would have been like.'

'That's what makes it so romantic — the fact that it has risen to such a peak and left us wanting more.'

'I read somewhere,' Lisa said reflectively, 'that these two movements are contrasts in mood: the storm and stress of life followed by serenity in which violence and heartache are only past memories.'

The look Andrew gave her was an odd mixture of surprise and admiration. He nodded. 'That describes it well. It has hidden depths. I would never have thought that you. . .' He stopped as he saw her stiffen. 'Don't fly at me. That's meant to be a compliment.'

'It sounded remarkably patronising to me,' Lisa retorted, then with a glint in her eyes she added, 'I can say the same thing about you. I would never have thought that you — the hard-boiled cynic — would have a romantic side to your character.'

'Cynical? Hard-boiled? Good heavens! Is that what you think I am?'

She nodded, and saw him wince. Then he leant forward.

'Lisa — you've got me all wrong. I'm not ——' He stopped, arrested by the sound of the telephone. 'Damn!' he said angrily and picked up the receiver.

The call, from what Lisa could make out, came from a nervous client seeking advice, and, while Andrew dealt with it calmly and expertly, she felt again that strange sensation, a sensation that grew as she watched his strong face and heard the deep voice sympathetically soothing his client's fears. Her heart began to pound as she realised what was happening to her. She was in love with him. In love with the man whom so recently she had disliked even to the point of hatred. It was shattering and for a few moments she sat absolutely rigid in her chair. Then, abruptly she stood up, resolved to take instant flight.

Turning, as he replaced the receiver, he looked surprised as she picked up her things. 'Don't go yet,' he said. 'That call was only for advice.'

She said hurriedly, 'I'm sorry but I must. I really have lots to do.'

In an effort to control her feelings, her manner became cool, almost distant, and he stared at her, obviously bewildered by her sudden change of mood. Going to the door, she said, 'Thank you for everything. I've enjoyed myself.' She fumbled for the door-handle, and as he reached past her to open it he said quietly, 'Another time, perhaps?'

She managed a smile, but looked away quickly as she saw he was still puzzled by her hasty departure. He little knew, she said to herself as she drove away, that she was running away against all her inclinations, running away from love — from a love that she felt sure would never be returned and that she must do her best to hide.

Back in her flat, she stood for a while in a kind of daze, not daring to look too deeply into her heart, and holding back desperately the storm of tears that threatened to overwhelm her. At last, seeing the chores that had to be done, she began mechanically to busy herself with practical things, hoping dully that routine work would help her to come to terms with what she knew to be an intolerable situation.

It was late when she finished, and by then she was able to face reality. Once more, however unwillingly, she had to make a complete U-turn. She must leave the practice. It was not possible to work alongside Andrew — she would never be able to disguise her feelings sufficiently to avoid them becoming noticeable. It would be too traumatic, make her too full of tension to do justice to her work. Of course, everyone would think she had gone off her head, and they wouldn't be far wrong. Love, and this *was* real love — unlike anything she had ever imagined — was a kind of madness. The saying 'madly in love' said it all. In a state of desperation she went to bed and lay awake for hours, dreading the coming weeks during which she must work out a month's notice. Suddenly she sat up in alarm as she remembered the partnership agreement which was presumably in the process of preparation. She must stop that immediately, and that meant she must tell Andrew tomorrow. James, too. . . Her heart sank even lower as she contemplated their reactions. Exhausted, she sank back on to the pillows. She couldn't even give a plausible reason for leaving. Perhaps tomorrow was too soon to tell them of her decision — it would take a little time to think up a good excuse, and at the moment she hadn't the faintest idea as to what she was going to say.

In the morning she awoke in a calmer frame of mind. Drained of all emotion, she was coldly firm in her resolution. Once she had made the break, she told herself, she would make another life for herself and try to stop crying for the moon. Accordingly, she worked steadily through a varied list of cases and even managed to take an interest in the nurses' conversation as they sat over coffee. She was so much in control of herself that even when Andrew came in she managed to greet him normally.

'I've got no appointments till eleven o'clock,' he said as he sat down. 'A lot of clients are going to the

Farmers' Union meeting, so I've got a nice quiet day — at least that's what I'm hoping.' As Sally put coffee in front of him he asked, 'Has Lisa told you about our new part-time assistant?'

'I'm sorry.' Lisa shook her head. 'I completely forgot. You tell them.'

He looked surprised. 'You must have a lot on your mind to forget such a pleasant piece of news. Well, this is the situation. . .'

When he had finished Sally said, 'Goodness, how exciting. When will he start?'

'He rang this morning. He's coming in for evening surgery today.' Turning to Lisa, he added, 'I'll take all the night calls until he knows his way around here, and then he and I will alternate.' He paused. 'We may have to take on another nurse, because the surgeries will go on longer. And another problem: Sally — are you really going to leave us?'

'Ah!' Sally flushed sheepishly, and glanced at Barbara. 'We've been talking, and Barbara has persuaded me to go to a day meeting for veterinary nurses over at Matford next Saturday. It's for first-year trainees. Lectures and question and answers — you know the kind of thing. I think I ought to go before I decide finally whether to change my career or not.' She looked at him doubtfully. 'My worry is how to get there. It begins at ten o'clock, and as I haven't got a car and there's no direct train I'd never get there in time.'

'Don't worry about that. We'll work something out. Perhaps Roger could take you.'

'Oh, goodness!' Sally looked a little shaken, then she frowned. 'It would mean spending the whole day there — I couldn't ask him to do that.'

Andrew laughed. 'He'll probably jump at the chance of escorting a pretty girl like you.'

Sally's eyes opened wide. 'Is he a bachelor? What does he look like?'

'He's not married. As for his appearance ——' he turned to Lisa with a mischievous smile '—perhaps you can help me out there. Would you say he's good-looking?' He grinned as she looked confused. 'I'll bet he could describe you—he couldn't keep his eyes off you—and no doubt you, with your strong powers of observation, can give a good description of him.'

Sally's face fell. 'Oh, well, if he is so keen on Lisa I haven't a chance.'

Lisa looked scornful. 'Don't take any notice of Andrew. He exaggerates everything. As for Roger— he's good-looking, very pleasant and, I imagine, very susceptible. When he sees you he'll probably be bowled right over.'

After that it was time for Lisa to operate, and Andrew went into the dispensary to collect the drugs for his case. When he emerged he stood for a few moments watching as she took up a scalpel preparatory to making an incision in the abdomen of an anaesthetised dog. Distracted by his presence, she looked up questioningly, and he said softly, 'How about this evening?'

Automatically, without thinking, she shook her head. 'Sorry, I can't. Thank you all the same.' Then, remembering with a sinking heart that she ought to have seized the occasion to tell of her new decision, she swallowed and began to speak, but, rebuffed, he had turned away. Telling herself that it was better to leave it at that, especially as she had not yet been able to think up a good excuse, she absorbed herself in her work. The nurses, she knew, were openly curious, but soon she forgot all about them as she concentrated on a difficult operation. At last, suturing up the wound, she gave a sigh of satisfaction.

'There! That should give him a new lease of life. That's the last patient, isn't it?' She paused. 'No, I can hear a car.'

Glancing out of the window, she said, 'Someone coming — it must be an emergency. Oh, dear —— ' she sighed ' — it's Mrs Tanner — I wonder what she's got for me this time.'

Barbara laughed and turned to Sally. 'She is a rather eccentric lady. She takes in all the weakest animals, birds et cetera, and tries to save them. Sometimes she does, then she keeps them in her large garden. She's very slow at paying her account — she has no money of her own, and her husband doesn't approve of having his orderly garden being taken over by all the weaklings of the animal world.'

Lisa smiled. 'Actually she's a very nice person. Her only fault is that her compassion is extreme. For instance, when one of her poor little pets is so ill that it ought to be put to sleep she seems unable to understand that it's cruel to keep it alive.'

At the sound of Mrs Tanner's entry into the waiting-room Sally went to open the door. She gave a small gasp as she glimpsed the head of a chicken peeping out from under a thick towel. She stood back as Mrs Tanner placed her bundle on the table and revealed a young hen in a state of distress. Her beak was opening and shutting as she gasped for breath, and occasionally she shook her head violently.

Her owner said dolefully, 'This dear little chicken was given me by someone who keeps hens. She was going to kill it, but I said I'd like to see if I could save her. That was yesterday, but she seems worse today. Do you think she's choking?'

Lisa nodded. 'Well, yes, in a way she is. She's got what is known as "the gapes". It's due to the presence of small worms in the bronchial tubes.' She looked down at the unfortunate bird. 'She's pretty bad. Don't you think it would be better to put her to sleep before she dies of exhaustion?'

'Oh, no!' Mrs Tanner's eyes filled with tears. 'She's such a sweet little bird, and I'm sure she trusts me to get her better. Surely with all these wonderful new drugs there must be something to give her?'

Lisa pondered. 'Well, there is something — thiabendazole — which is effective in the early stages. Unfortunately she's pretty far gone.' She went over to the drug cupboard and took out a packet. 'You put this powder in the bird's drinking water — that's if she's still able to drink.'

Mrs Tanner took it eagerly. 'I'll get it down her somehow.'

'The instructions are on the packet,' Lisa said, 'and if you succeed in saving her I'd be pleased if you would let me know. By the way, she must be kept in isolation, and if she recovers or dies the cage in which you keep her must be thoroughly disinfected.'

Mrs Tanner fumbled in her purse, then looked up helplessly. 'How much do I owe you?'

Lisa smiled. 'Let's see if you can save her first. The treatment should work quickly, so don't let her go on suffering if you don't see any improvement very soon. In that case, if you can't do it yourself, I'll put her to sleep.'

Mrs Tanner thanked her gratefully, then, with an apologetic smile, she said, 'I suppose you think I'm far too sentimental. My husband says I am. The fact is I can't bear to see any living thing in trouble without wanting to put it right.' She paused. 'I often sit up all night nursing any pet animal if it's off colour.'

'I know how you feel —' Lisa nodded sympathetically ' — but there are times, you know, when it's kinder to put them peacefully to sleep.'

Mrs Tanner nodded solemnly, but it was plain to see that she was not persuaded, and when she had gone Sally said, 'Goodness! I hope I never get like that. She must be very uncomfortable to live with. I pity her poor husband.'

'Grounds for divorce, I should think,' said Barbara.

When the laughter had subsided Lisa went into the office, but before settling down to paperwork she sat deep in thought. How and when was she going to break her news to Andrew? It must be soon—perhaps she ought to ring him and tell him she would see him this evening after all. As for giving him a reason—she thrust the problem aside and decided to rely on inspiration when the time came. And that time must be this evening.

CHAPTER EIGHT

FOR the rest of the day Lisa was uneasy. Distracted by worry over the need to give in her notice, she found it difficult to concentrate on her work. This fact alone made it only too clear that she had made the right decision so, having finished her evening meal, she picked up the telephone with a shaking hand.

Andrew was obviously pleased when she said she would like to see him.

'I'm glad you've changed your mind. I've got some new compact discs — I'd like your opinion.'

Swallowing hard, Lisa said, 'Actually I don't want to listen to records. I need to talk to you about — ' she hesitated ' — well, about me. I'll be with you soon.'

Half an hour later, having given her decision, she sat, stiff with misery, as he exploded with anger.

'You must be crazy! For God's sake, Lisa, what's the matter with you? First you won't take a partnership, then you will, and now you won't. I know it's a woman's privilege to change her mind, but this is ludicrous!' He drew a long breath, passed his hand across his forehead. 'It beats all. I can understand your initial refusal — that was when we were at loggerheads — but since we've sorted all that out I thought everything was going to be straightforward from now on. Now I'm completely floored.'

He got up and stood looking down at her, his expression a mixture of bewilderment and exasperation, and her heart sank. He must indeed think she was unbalanced. She could hardly blame him. At last, as she remained silent, he asked sharply, 'Aren't you going to tell me your reasons for your change of heart?'

She thought wildly, Change of heart — that sums it all up. The one reason I can't give him. In her turn she stood up and faced him.

'I'm sorry — I really am very sorry — but there it is. I must leave. I don't even want to stay as an assistant. I need to get away.'

Suddenly, to her dismay, he put his hands on her shoulders.

'But that's not enough. Why do you need to get away? What's troubling you, Lisa?' The anger had gone from his eyes and now they were full of compassion, and his voice was warm and friendly.

Helplessly she shook her head, longing to confide in him but knowing that this was the one thing she could never do.

'I can't possibly explain.' Her voice trembled. 'It's just everything. I'm not happy here, that's all.'

He searched her face as though endeavouring to read her mind, then suddenly he released his grip on her shoulders and stepped back, his mouth set in a grim line.

'It's me, isn't it? You needn't flush up like that. I understand only too well. You just don't like me. I'm the man who bullied and insulted you and with whom you can never really be at ease.'

She wanted to cry out, No! You've got it all wrong. You've misunderstood me as you always do. Then suddenly her mind cleared. It was better this way. This could be her real reason for leaving, and not even James or Angela would be able to dissuade her. No matter that it made her appear hard and too proud to forgive and forget. It was the only way out for her. She drew a long, unhappy breath and nodded slowly, watching sadly as the colour drained from his face.

He said harshly, 'So that's it. Just as I was beginning to think. . .' He stopped abruptly, then he added grimly, 'Well, never mind that. I was wrong.' His eyes were bleak and cold, and Lisa felt she wanted to die. In a daze she heard him say, 'Very well. I'll explain to James and Angela that this time your decision is irrevocable, and I'll keep out of your way as much as possible.'

Lisa stood very still for a few moments, then, with the feeling that she was living in a nightmare, she moved slowly towards the door.

'Wait!' The urgency in his voice made her turn. 'I have an idea. There's no reason for you to leave — to chuck up the partnership that you deserve. No — don't shake your head.' He sounded almost desperate. 'You must listen. I'll go instead. After all, I'm the newcomer in the practice. I'm the one who has caused all the trouble. Someone can take my place — Roger, perhaps. He'd jump at it, and I know he could afford to buy a half-share.' He stopped, drew a long breath, then said, 'That's the right way to do things. It's the solution to your problem.'

Her mouth went dry and she gasped, 'I couldn't possibly — I can't agree to that.'

'Why not?' He stared at her fiercely, then as she seemed too bewildered to answer he added, 'You must agree. I insist. Your partnership here can go through with another name substituted for mine.' He waited, but still she said nothing, then, as though speaking to himself, he said quietly, 'I'll probably go back to Canada. There's nothing to hold me here.'

Lisa stood in numbed silence. The tables were turned on her, and although Andrew's plan was all to her advantage she felt shattered. He had taken everything out of her hands. Her face must have showed her distress, for he said,

'What's wrong now? Why do you look so troubled? Surely you should be glad? Your life can go on smoothly—I shan't be here to rub you up the wrong way. As for me, well——' He paused and she saw a vein throb in his temple '—I'll survive and hope you will forgive me for causing you so much unhappiness.' He reached out and once more put his hands on her shoulders. 'Will you, Lisa?' She stiffened involuntarily, and almost immediately he released her, saying grimly, 'Oh, God! That's all I need to know. The way you react when I touch you—you make it so plain that you loathe me.'

'Please—I don't—you shouldn't think that. . .' She looked up at him imploringly, but he misread the appeal in her eyes.

He said bitterly, 'I've been a fool. Messed things up completely. Well, at least I can stop you from throwing away your big chance.'

At last Lisa found her voice. 'There's no need for you to do anything so drastic. James will be far more upset at losing you than me. He can't possibly find a partner to replace you so soon. He knows nothing about Roger, but he does know you. Your father was his closest friend. A complete stranger would have to work here for a long time before he could prove he was suitable to take your place. It would be——'

'Stop making difficulties.' He cut her short. 'I'll sort things out with James.' He gave her a long, sad look, and under his gaze the colour drained from her face. She wanted to burst into tears, she wanted to tell him that he had got everything wrong, but it was no use. With a helpless shrug she turned to the door. This time he let her go, and her heart felt like lead as he closed the door behind her.

Next day she saw him only when he came into the surgery for essentials and refused invitations to coffee

under the pretext of pressure of work. Trying to overcome her feeling of desolation, she joined in the nurses'
conversation and endeavoured to keep up her pretence
of normality. Asking Sally what she thought of Roger
Ballard, she could not help smiling when the other girl
burst out,

'Oh, he's brilliant! Fantastic! A bit nervous at first,
but that was only natural. He soon relaxed and was the
most tremendous fun.'

Barbara laughed as she exchanged amused glances
with Lisa. 'She's got it badly this time.' More seriously
she added, 'He's certainly very nice, and he went down
well with the clients.'

'He's going to take me to the nurses' lecture day on
Saturday.' Sally flushed, then added hesitatingly, 'You
don't mind, Lisa, do you?'

Lisa stared. 'For goodness' sake! Why on earth
should I mind?'

'Well from what Andrew said——'

'Rubbish!' Lisa said scornfully. 'Absolute nonsense.
You go ahead, Sally, but. . .'

She paused, and Barbara finished the phrase for her.
'Just be careful this time.'

Sally frowned. 'This is different. I'm sure Roger isn't
the type to—well, you know what I mean.'

'On the strength of your very short acquaintance I
don't see how you can judge a man's character so
accurately,' Lisa said drily, and wondered for a moment
why the two nurses exchanged glances. It was only,
later, when she was alone, that she recalled her sarcastic
words and applied them to herself. She had judged
Andrew at first as an intolerant bully, but how wrong
she had been.

Throughout the following week the only conversation
she had with Andrew was purely professional. There
had been no word from either James or Angela, so she

supposed that Andrew had not yet told them of his decision to leave. He was probably waiting for the right moment, which might not be until the wording of the partnership agreement had been settled. It was a depressing week, made even worse when, on the day that Andrew was due at Mr Marsden's farm to take the stitches out of the injured ewe, Olivia, coming in for some worm tablets for her cat, announced that she was going with him.

'To choose a kitten,' she said gleefully. 'A nice outing with an attractive man.'

Intercepting a quick glance between Barbara and Sally, Lisa could only smile as Olivia went away, but inwardly she felt a sharp pang. No matter that Andrew said he didn't like Olivia — one only had to think of her provocative manner to fear the worst.

Then, in the middle of evening surgery, Andrew appeared.

'Those kittens aren't thriving,' he said. 'They obviously aren't getting enough milk. I've given the mother an injection, but Mrs Marsden would like your opinion and wants you to go over tomorrow morning after surgery. 'I'll meet you there about eleven-thirty.'

There was nothing for it but to agree, and as she set out next day she tried to keep calm by concentrating on the cat and her kittens. On arrival at the farm she saw Andrew's car in the yard and, pulling up beside it, she braced herself. She must not betray her feelings towards him, and this would be a good test.

As he strolled across to greet her she sat very still, held immobile by the thoughts flooding into her mind — thoughts that were difficult to control. He looked so handsome and so infinitely dear to her that she began to tremble. He seemed like a man who was completely heart-free, and for that state of mind she envied him. Perhaps, she thought despondently, when he had gone out of her life she would eventually be able to think of him with cool indifference, but as he drew near and she got out of her car to meet him she knew with a quick flash of intuition that she would never be able to forget him, never be able to tear him from her heart.

Something of her unhappiness must have shown in her face, for he looked at her searchingly.

'Anything wrong, Lisa? Was it difficult to get away from the surgery?'

'No, no. Everything there is under control,' she said. 'I was just thinking about this cat. Has she no milk at all?'

'Only enough to feed one kitten, and she's got five.'

Ushered into the farmhouse kitchen and greeted thankfully by Mrs Marsden, Lisa examined the mother cat carefully. At last she shrugged regretfully.

Mrs Marsden shook her head slowly, then said practically, 'Well, we must decide what to do about the kittens.' She turned to Andrew. 'Your friend—Mrs Claydon—who came yesterday—does she still want one?'

He nodded. 'I think so, but then you want one for yourself, don't you?'

'Yes, I do,' she said decidedly, 'and I've got a friend who will take one and rear it by hand, though it's a difficult task. I don't suppose Mrs Claydon would be able to cope with such a time-consuming routine—feeding every two hours night and day for about three weeks—so she'll have to look elsewhere.'

'I've already told her the situation,' said Andrew, 'but she said she wanted to see for herself. She should be here soon.'

As he spoke, Olivia's car turned into the yard, and a few minutes later she astonished them all by declaring that she would like to try her hand at rearing the kitten of her choice.

'I know it's difficult,' she said calmly, 'but I'm sure David will help me, and with you two——' she looked at Lisa and Andrew '—I'm sure I'll succeed.'

Lisa gazed at her incredulously. What was she trying to prove? Was she out to prove her devotion to animals and at the same time involve both Andrew and David?

Once more Mrs Marsden spoke practically. 'Well, that leaves two to be put down. The two smallest and weakest. . .' She looked at Lisa. 'I'll leave that to you.'

Olivia gave a sudden wail. 'Oh, how awful! I can't bear. . . I must go. I'll get the necessary things for feeding my kitten, then I'll come back and fetch it.'

She went off hurriedly, and Lisa, swallowing hard, got down to her sad task. Then Mrs Marsden said, 'Come in and have some coffee. You deserve a drink.'

Andrew shook his head. Lisa also declined, and as they walked towards their respective cars Andrew said, 'Would you like to come with me? A couple of calls—a change from small animals.' He saw her stare of astonishment and shrugged. 'Of course, if you'd rather not. . . I thought you might be interested.'

'Oh, but I would,' she said quickly. 'It's kind of you to suggest it. Sometimes I regret the fact that I don't have the opportunity to do farm work. It's not easy to break down the farmers' resistance to women vets.'

Mrs Marsden, coming up behind them, laughed heartily.

'That's true. My Bob is so stuck in his ways you wouldn't believe. But there, men are all the same. You just have to accept them as they are.' She paused as they stood politely waiting to say goodbye. 'You two seem to get on very well. I suppose doing the same kind of work makes a bond between you.' She gave a mischievous smile. 'A good basis for marriage.' She burst out laughing. 'If you could see your faces! You mustn't mind me. My Bob says I'm too outspoken by

far. But I find people interesting, especially young ones
like you two. I know I've put my foot into what isn't
my business, but what I say is, who lives longest will
see the most.' She gave another chuckle, then said,
'Well, I must go and see about those kittens. I expect
your friend will soon be back to collect hers.'

When she was out of earshot Andrew said, 'Nosey
old girl. Still, she's a good sort.' He glanced at Lisa as
she opened her car door. 'Embarrassed you, didn't
she?'

Lisa shrugged, then, settling herself behind the
wheel, she asked, 'Where's your first call?'

'Bennett's pig farm. A routine check. We'll probably
get asked in for a coffee. That's why I didn't accept Mrs
Marsden's offer. Then I've got some pregnancy diagnoses at Willow Farm. How's that?'

Lisa was pleased, and as she drove behind Andrew
she marvelled at the strange relationship between them.
They were drawn together by their common interest
but held apart by so many misunderstandings. Recalling
Andrew's decision to leave the practice, she was suddenly overcome by the enormity of his sacrifice. She
couldn't possibly accept it, and must somehow persuade
him that there was no need for him to go. This morning
had convinced her that it was perfectly possible to work
alongside him without betraying her love for him. The
prospect of never seeing him again was too terrible to
contemplate. But how to persuade him that she wanted
him to stay without betraying her real feelings? That
problem she had yet to solve.

Suddenly she noticed that Andrew was signalling a
left turn and, after driving up a rough lane, she pulled
up behind him in a large yard. As they walked toward
the farmhouse door she said quickly, 'Andrew — I
must have a talk with you. It's important, so when
and where?'

He glanced at her in surprise. 'OK. We'll take a break as soon as I've finished here.' He paused, his hand on the heavy door-knocker. 'Just listen to that noise. They must be having some sort of party. Most unusual. Not like the Bennett family at all.'

Mr Bennett himself opened the door and, glimpsing the number of people inside, Andrew said quickly, 'I rather think we've come at the wrong time. You won't want to abandon your party and go out to the pigs. I'll come tomorrow if that's all right with you.'

'No, certainly not. Come along in. It's the pigs that are the cause of our celebration.' Mr Bennett's jovial face beamed as he drew them in and, after Andrew had hurriedly introduced Lisa, he led them through the crush of people towards the window. It overlooked a large field in which about forty pigs were happily rooting around.

Lisa said, 'That's nice—pigs allowed to run free instead of being confined in sties.'

Mr Bennett nodded. 'And thereby hangs a tale. Lots of curly tails, in fact. The battle we've had with the people who've moved into those new houses—you can see them at the far end of the field—we've won it at last. Let me get you a drink, then I'll tell you about it.'

A few minutes later he unfolded his story. 'We decided to abandon intensive production and go in for natural methods. So we put the fences in good order and turned the pigs out into this field. They're flourishing, as you can see. Then suddenly the complaints came flooding in.' He pointed to the houses. 'Yuppies— townies—they objected to having pigs on their boundaries. They obtained an injunction preventing us from keeping pigs within two hundred yards. The builders said they were having difficulties in selling the houses, and a writ was served against us claiming damages. So we started our own legal action, and thankfully the

High Court found in our favour. The judge said we had
shown no malice in setting up our outdoor pig enter-
prise and that people who come to live in the countryside must be prepared to put up with animals — smells
and whatever.' He laughed. 'Believe it or not, lots of
those people over there profess themselves to be great
animal lovers — some are even members of animal
liberation societies — but when it came to letting pigs
live freely near their own houses. . .that was a different
story. Bunch of hypocrites.' He paused. 'Have another
drink.'

Laughingly they refused, and with Andrew's promise
to return next day they managed to get away. As they
reached their cars Andrew glanced at his watch and
said, 'Well, now we've got a bit of time. I'm not due at
my next call for half an hour, so let's park our cars
somewhere down the lane. Then you tell me what's on
you mind. Better still, as it's such a nice day we'll go
for a walk.'

Lisa hesitated. Now that she had the opportunity to
tell him of her new idea she felt unaccountably nervous.
But there was no avoiding it, so, bracing herself, she
nodded assent, and as she drove down the rough track
to the main road she began to rehearse a way in which
to express her thoughts.

A few minutes later they walked slowly down a path
leading into a wood. At first they spoke casually of the
beauty of the autumnal colours, then, as they came
upon a fallen log, Andrew said, 'Let's sit here. Now
what's the trouble?'

It was difficult for her to find the right words, but at
last she began haltingly to tell him of her new idea.

Gazing at her incredulously, he listened in silence,
but as soon as she had finished he shook his head as
though bewildered and then burst out laughing.

Indignantly she turned to stare at him. 'I'm perfectly

serious. There's no need for either of us to leave the practice. What's funny about that?'

He checked himself with difficulty. 'Funny? Why it's ridiculous! I'm getting positively giddy with all your U-turns.'

She flushed and looked away, unable to face the derision in his eyes. She shrugged. 'I'm sorry you see it that way. I just thought that we were both making a mountain out of a molehill, but if you think I'm so changeable and indecisive than it's obvious that a partnership with you wouldn't work.' She rose to her feet. 'Forget it. I'm sorry I said anything.'

She began to walk back to the lane, but he got up quickly and pulled her back. Forcing her round towards him, he studied her face seriously and his grip tightened.

'Lisa, I'm sorry too. I didn't mean to upset you. Of course you're right. We've both been acting like silly children. Time to grow up.'

Gazing up at him, her whole body afire at his touch, Lisa knew full well that she had indeed grown up—a painful process that involved the real suffering of unrequited love.

Suddenly his hands dropped from her shoulders and he stepped back. 'Why do you look at me like that?' Then, answering his own question, he said grimly, 'You don't like me touching you, do you? I must remember that.' There was silence while he frowned, deep in thought, and she gazed back at him in speechless dismay.

At last she said, 'No, it's not that—you're wrong. . .'

He interrupted harshly, 'No, I'm not. I understand perfectly. Physically you dislike me—that's very obvious—but intellectually, professionally, we could make successful partners. You're right there. There's no reason for either of us to change course.' He smiled wryly and said, 'Let's be businesslike and shake hands.'

She put out her hand reluctantly, knowing that his touch would electrify her, and his mouth twisted momentarily.

'Do I repel you so much that you can't even shake hands?'

Goaded into anger, she said fiercely, 'Don't be so foolish, Andrew. I said just now that you've got it all wrong. I don't dislike you. I did at first, but I've put all that behind me. But you always misunderstand me, and perhaps that's why I've been so indecisive. I never know how you're going to react.'

His eyes searched her face once more, then slowly he smiled.

'So we can wipe out past mistakes and start all over again?'

She nodded and, meeting his eyes, she saw in them an expression that made her heart beat unevenly. For a moment she felt an upsurge of hope, but quickly she forced it down. She mustn't delude herself. He was only offering friendship, and with that she must be content.

He glanced at his watch. 'We must go. Mustn't keep old Mr Forster waiting. He's a crusty old farmer, but a good client. Don't take offence if he makes uncomplimentary remarks about women vets. He takes pride in not moving with the times.'

Mr Forster was all that Andrew had said, and when he learnt who Lisa was he pursed his lips and gazed at her frowningly.

'Well, you can come and watch, of course, but I don't see why a woman vet should need to know anything about farm animals.'

Pulling on his obstetric gown, Andrew said coolly, 'Miss Benson is just as capable as I am. She could do these pregnancy diagnoses as well as I can. She's had the same training, you know.'

Mr Forster was not convinced. 'Training is one thing; putting it into practice is another. And I still think it's a bit unpleasant to see a young lady doing dirty work like this.'

Lisa opened her mouth, then shut it quickly as Andrew rose to her defence.

'In hospitals all over the world women doctors and nurses are doing equally unpleasant work on humans.' He grinned at the farmer. 'I'm sure that if no male vet were available to treat one of your animals in an emergency and a woman vet came along you'd be surprised at her efficiency.'

Mr Forster said nothing for a few moments, then he shrugged and said slowly, 'Maybe. What you're saying is that I'm old-fashioned.'

'Certainly not in your farming methods, Mr Forster,' Lisa said firmly. 'These cows look in the peak of condition, and from what I saw as I drove in your farm must be one of the cleanest, tidiest ones in the county.'

He looked at her sharply and grinned reluctantly. 'Flattery, young lady. But I do pride myself on keeping my farm up to the mark.' He turned to look at Andrew, who was working steadily through the line of cows. 'When he's finished that lot, we'll go in and have a cup of coffee.'

It was when they were chatting amicably in the farmhouse kitchen that a call came through from the surgery to go to a farm near by where a cow was having a difficult calving. After taking down the details, Andrew asked, 'Is Lisa needed in the surgery? No? OK. In that case she'll be with me, assisting with the calving.'

Lisa felt a glow of pleasure. 'Are you sure you don't

mind me trailing around with you? I find it awfully interesting, of course.'

'Thought you might. This farm is only about two miles from here. The road is narrow and winds a lot, do drive carefully.'

Mr Forster laughed. 'There you are! Just like me! Old fashioned enough not to trust women drivers.' He grinned broadly as Lisa began to protest. 'My daughter says I'm a male chauvinist pig.' He chuckled. 'I don't mind being called that a bit. Pigs are highly intelligent animals.'

As they drove away Lisa waved to the still laughing farmer and smiled to herself as she followed Andrew down the drive. This was turning out to be a very pleasant outing. It was good to get away from the confines of the surgery and see the other side of veterinary work. She said as much to Andrew when they pulled up in the next farmyard. Changing once more into his boots and obstetric gown, he nodded.

'Mind you, it's often hard physical work. This calving will probably be a good example. Nowadays herdsmen don't call in the vet for normal calvings. It's only when things are tricky that they need us.' He paused. 'Look — I haven't got another gown so you'd better put on that overall. It's a bit large for you, but it will protect your clothes.'

Mr Bridges, the farmer, was looking very depressed.

'She's been straining for four hours. One foot came out then went back in again. Since then, nothing. She keeps trying, and now she's getting very tired.'

Andrew began his examination and at last he said, 'Yes — there's the foot, but where the other one is. . . Ah, I've found it. Folded back. I'll have to straighten it out. The head is lying right back too.' He withdrew his arm. 'I'll give her an injection to stop the straining while I work the head forward.'

Mr Bridges glanced at Lisa. 'I expect you'd like a cup of tea, miss. My wife is in the kitchen — she'll be glad to see you.'

Lisa smiled. 'Thank you, but I'm too interested to leave. Besides, I can probably help. Having had that spinal injection, she's not going to give Andrew any help herself.'

Andrew spoke over his shoulder. 'Where's your herdsman? I should have thought——'

'He's in bed with flu,' Mr Bridges said gloomily. 'He wanted to come out here, but he's got a temperature, so I said no.'

'Well, he couldn't have done anything,' said Andrew cheerfully. 'This is a vet's job.'

Fascinated, Lisa watched as Andrew got down on his knees and began his difficult task. With her own knowledge she understood fully what he was doing and the physical strength involved. It took some time and she was relieved when he said at last,

'That's it. Everything is straightened out. Now for the calf ropes. Lisa, will you help Mr Bridges, please? I've got to guide the head out.'

Being an Angus calf, it was fairly small, and it didn't take much pulling to get the shoulder out. The rest followed easily, and as the calf fell on to the straw Mr Bridges said jubilantly, 'A fine little heifer. Thank you, Mr Morland; nice work.'

Gently Andrew dragged the little bundle up to its mother's head, Mr Bridges pulled the release knot on the rope, and with a soft moo of pleasure the gentle animal gave her baby a little nudge, then began licking it all over with her rough tongue.

'That will stimulate its breathing,' said Andrew and straightened his back with a long sigh of relief.

Cleaned up and refreshed with a quick cup of tea, Andrew and Lisa went back to their cars. Opening his door, Andrew said, 'I'm so hungry I could eat a horse — not a very good veterinary attitude, but I could certainly do with a sandwich or something. There's a pub in the village — shall we drop in there?'

The early autumn sunshine was still warm enough for them to sit outside and enjoy a ploughman's lunch. Having selected a wooden table and bench in a quiet part of the garden, they ate for a while in companionable silence. A squirrel, searching among the windfalls from an old apple tree, froze for a moment at the sight of intruders, then darted away. Lisa laughed, threw a piece of cheese in his direction, and watched as he made a quick dash, picked it up, and made off again. Looking up, she met Andrew's steady gaze. Some swift emotion flashed into his eyes, then he blinked as though coming out of a dream. Passing his hand through his dark hair, which was already ruffled by the slight breeze, he said,

'You know, you're very like that squirrel: very elusive, always on your guard. But unlike the squirrel you seem to have a protective shell around you — more like a hermit crab.'

Lisa burst out laughing. 'A squirrel! A hermit crab! Is that how you see me? I must say I've never been summed up so unflatteringly.'

He chuckled. 'Well, maybe I could have chosen better metaphors.' He paused. 'A beautiful young fawn hiding in the woods — that's more like it, perhaps. You certainly hide yourself from the world. You're still suffering from the trauma of your broken engagement, aren't you?'

The blunt question took her aback, and she stopped laughing. Picking up her glass, she took a quick sip then shook her head decisively.

'No. That's all over. I feel only a great sense of relief

that I escaped from what would, I'm absolutely sure, have been a very unhappy marriage.'

He looked doubtful. 'I think the experience left its mark on you, all the same. Do you think you will ever fall in love again?'

Lisa frowned. 'I've already told you — what I felt for Derek wasn't love at all.' Cautiously she added, 'As for the future, how can I tell?' Then impulsively she asked, 'What about you? Are you searching for someone?' She saw his eyebrows rise, and quickly turned the conversation into a joke. 'What about a pretty girl like Sally? Or a smart, sophisticated woman like Olivia?'

It was his turn to laugh. 'Are you matchmaking for me? If so, you're on the wrong track.' He grinned mockingly. 'According to Mrs Marsden, you and I have a great bond between us, which she says is a good basis for marriage. Do you agree with her?'

Lisa caught her breath. This was dangerous ground. She managed to say scornfully, 'Very practical, but most unromantic. Rather like a business merger.' Then, glancing at her watch, she added, 'I really ought to go back now. Thank you for taking me round this morning. I've enjoyed it immensely. I wish. . .' She paused, then shrugged resignedly, 'No use crying for the moon. I'm a small-animal vet and that's that.'

Andrew looked thoughtful. 'Oh, I don't know. I don't see why you shouldn't take on some farm work if you want to. We could work out something when Roger becomes full-time, as I'm pretty sure he will.'

Her eyes widened. 'Goodness! That's a marvellous idea. I'd love to work for — say — a couple of farms. That is, of course, if the farmers would accept me. Do you think that's possible?'

'Anything is possible.' He smiled. 'A bit of gentle persuasion, a few jobs done satisfactorily. . . I don't see why we shouldn't convert them.'

She said nothing, but her eyes showed so much gratitude that Andrew said, 'No need to be humble about it. You're an equal partner, remember, and half the practice is yours. We two can put through any changes we like so long as we both agree.'

With a sudden lift of her heart, Lisa felt that the future no longer seemed quite so depressing. It was obvious that Andrew would never be more than a friend—that she must learn to accept—but her work would become more interesting. Absorbed and busy, she would not have time to indulge in dreams that would never come true.

CHAPTER NINE

BACK in the surgery Lisa longed for solitude so that she could reflect on all that had happened, but there was no time for that. Suddenly it was all go.

A dog came in with a broken leg which had to be set, a bitch who was unable to produce her puppies needed a Caesarean operation, and the afternoon passed quickly. Soon there were so many people in the waiting-room that it was plain to see that evening surgery was going to be equally busy.

Halfway through, much to Lisa's relief, Roger appeared to take over, and Sally, who had been on the point of rebellion at working late, immediately decided to stay on. Lisa smiled wistfully as she went up to her flat. Romance was in the air as far as those two were concerned. It was to be hoped that all would go smoothly and that Sally would not end up sadly disillusioned once more. Roger seemed to have succumbed to her charm, but was he the faithful type? Her thoughts turned to Andrew, in spite of a valiant effort to stop him taking over her mind. Was he the faithful type? He had said he wanted a love that would last a lifetime. She sighed. How wonderful to be the one who aroused such feelings in him. But that, she told herself, was just a fantasy. It was no good indulging in daydreams. She seemed to be fated to be a loser in love. Was she, she wondered unhappily, her own worst enemy? Andrew had told her she was encased in a protective shell like a hermit crab, and although it was a joke there was so much truth in it that she winced at the picture it conjured up. He little knew that he was the only man who could draw her out of her self-imposed captivity. He was her ideal, mentally and physically. No other man would ever measure up to him, but their unfortunate first encounter had left a trail of misunderstandings in its wake. And now she must be constantly on her guard against betraying her love for him. Something like despair swept over her, and for a few minutes she let her tears flow. At last, ashamed of having indulged in self-pity, she bathed her eyes and surveyed herself in the mirror. Her reflection was still tear-stained, but with no one to see it really didn't matter.

Then suddenly, as though to contradict her, the telephone rang insistently.

'Lisa——' Olivia's voice was full of panic '—I'm having trouble with this kitten. He seems to be fading away. I rang Andrew, but he said I should contact you.'

'Yes, of course. Bring him to my flat—Roger is doing the late surgery.' Lisa replaced the receiver, glanced quickly once more in the mirror, hoping fervently that Olivia would be so absorbed in her kitten that she wouldn't see the signs of an emotional upset.

It was as she thought, for Olivia was so worked up that she noticed nothing, and she waited, breathing fast, while Lisa examined the kitten. It took only a minute to see that nothing could be done to save the sad little creature, and Lisa shook her head slowly. 'I'm afraid——' she began, and Olivia burst out,

'Don't tell me there's no hope. I've done my best. In fact I'm quite worn out. I've fed him regularly, but he takes less and less. David has been helping me, and he's very good and patient, but he thinks it's serious now. I told him I was bringing him to you and he said he'd join me here. Lisa—isn't there anything you can do?'

Then, just as Lisa was contemplating, the kitten turned its head feebly and lay still. So still that even

Olivia recognised the signs. Lisa looked up and said gently, 'I'm sorry. It's not your fault, so don't blame yourself.'

'But I do,' Olivia wailed. 'I should have brought him to you sooner — you might have saved him.'

'No, I honestly don't think I could have.' Absorbed in trying to comfort the other girl, Lisa scarcely realised that her doorbell was ringing.

'That will be David. . .' Olivia wiped her eyes and went across to the mirror, while Lisa, still holding the kitten, went to the door.

David took one glance at the tiny body, then went straight to Olivia and took her in his arms. It took some time to calm her down, but gradually, after a recuperative drink, she recovered and, comforted by David's promise that he would help her to find another kitten, she went away with him.

It was while Lisa was standing at the window watching them drive away that she saw Andrew's car turning into the yard. Trying to quell her fast-beating heart as she heard him coming up the stairs, she opened the door and said, 'The kitten is dead and I'm afraid Olivia is distraught.'

'Yes,' he said, 'I saw them as they left here.' He paused. 'May I come in?'

She looked surprised but held the door open, and he said, 'I didn't come earlier because I guessed the kitten was on the way out. I just wanted to make sure that you haven't been made to feel responsible.'

'Oh, no. Actually Olivia blamed herself, but it was really no one's fault. I did my best to reassure her. She had obviously done her best.'

He nodded, then, glancing at the glasses on the table, he said lightly, 'Are you going to be as hospitable to me as you were to them?'

She flushed. 'Of course. What would you like?'

'A coffee, please,' he said promptly and followed her into the kitchen. As they waited for the kettle to boil he said quietly, 'Actually, I really came to apologise.'

Astonished, she stared at him. 'What on earth for?'

'For calling you a hermit crab. A horrible little creature, and one you don't resemble in the least.'

She dissolved into laughter. 'Of all the ridiculous excuses. . .' she began, and he chuckled.

'Well, yes. It was an excuse, but I really did feel uncomfortable about the unflattering comparison.'

Pouring out the coffee, she said coolly, 'I don't want flattery. It's never sincere. As a matter of fact, I've come to the conclusion that you were right.'

He looked at her searchingly and, remembering her recent tears, she flushed.

'So I did upset you,' he said, and the sympathy in his voice caused a lump to rise in her throat.

But she managed a shrug and said lightly, 'No, really. I was more upset by the kitten's death. Poor Olivia was shattered.'

'She'll find comfort in David's arms,' Andrew said drily. 'I think those two will make a match of it—very romantic.'

'Precious little romance about it,' Lisa said caustically. 'David just wants an intelligent, attractive woman.' She paused, trying to recall his words. 'He told me he didn't believe in romantic love. Affection—mutual interests—that's what he wants. He's purely practical.'

'He told you this?' Andrew stared. 'Was that a proposal?'

'I suppose you could call it that,' Lisa said lightly. 'He asked me if there was a man in my life, and when I said no he asked if he could fill the vacancy.'

'Good lord! Just like offering you a job. Well, I pity Olivia, then. She's going to be disappointed in him.'

'No, I don't think she will be. Underneath all that
gush she's practical too. She admires David, he's very
prosperous, travels a lot and, like her is very fond of
cats. I think they're well matched. They'll be happy.
After all, they're both divorced, and I've heard it said
that second time round is often very successful.'

He said drily, 'I thought you didn't believe that mere
compatibility was enough.'

'Not for me.' Lisa kept her voice steady. 'It's sometimes enough for others, and who's to say they're not
the most sensible ones in the end?'

He gazed at her intently and she looked back steadfastly. Then he said, 'So once again we're back to Mrs
Marsden — remember? A bond between two people is
a good basis for marriage. That's what you're saying,
isn't it?'

'Sometimes. But as I've said, it's not for me.'

'Nor for me. Love may occasionally come after
marriage, but it's a terrible risk to take. And that makes
it a point in favour of living together in order to make
sure. Are you in favour of that kind of relationship?'

She hesitated. 'Not really. Very often people go from
one partner to another until in the end they find it
impossible to distinguish between. . .'

She stopped and, smiling a little cynically, he finished
her phrase. 'Love and lust. Are you too inhibited to put
it so bluntly?'

She flushed angrily. 'I'm not inhibited.'

He laughed grimly. 'Oh, yes, you are, you know. I
begin to think that even if you fell deeply in love you
would be too fearful to let yourself go.'

It was more than she could stand. Not wanting him
to see her agitation, she stood up quickly.

'Andrew — I'm going to turn you out. I've got several
chores to do and it's been a long day.'

He rose slowly. 'Well, that's as good a reason as any

for breaking up a conversation that troubles you.' Without warning he put his hands on her shoulders and, when she automatically drew back, his grip tightened.

He said very quietly, 'I would like to kiss you, but I'm held back by your resistance, or should I say your inhibitions?' He paused. 'Perhaps, though, it's because you still dislike me.'

Although her whole being yearned towards him, she still held back. There was a flame in his eyes, but, she told herself, it was only an expression of physical desire. Desire without love was worthless, and if she yielded to his undoubted attraction she would surely betray herself and he would be startled and embarrassed. Sadly she saw the flame in his eyes slowly fade, and he said harshly, as he let her go, 'I'm sorry. I keep forgetting, although you make it plain enough. I repel you.'

She wanted to cry out, to tell him how terribly wrong he was, but instead she said coolly, 'No need to be so dramatic. We're friends, but there's no necessity to be so demonstrative.'

He winced. 'God! What an iceberg! Just when I was beginning to think. . .' He stopped abruptly, then as he turned away he said, 'I've been a fool.'

The door slammed behind him and, petrified, Lisa stood motionless. What had she done? What did he mean? Had she killed a love for her that she had never suspected? In a kind of daze she began to pace the room, his bitter words echoing in her ears. Her heart seemed turned to stone as, exhausted by emotion, she managed to go through the routine of getting ready for bed and lay awake till the early hours.

In the morning she acknowledged dully that there was no way back. She had made a ghastly mistake and would have to live with it. A malignant fate seemed to have singled her out for unhappiness.

Morning surgery was busy, and the nurses seemed not to notice that she was distracted and uncertain, though Barbara looked at her curiously from time to time. With a longing to be alone, she declined coffee and went up to her flat. Her mouth felt so dry that she poured herself a glass of mineral water, but before she had a chance to drink it the telephone rang.

Olivia, her sorrow at the kitten's death apparently forgotten, said, 'Lisa—I just want to let you know that, if you and Andrew are giving any consideration to my idea of working in your practice forget it, please. I've changed my mind. I hope. . .' She paused. 'Well, you'll understand when David and I give you our news. I won't say any more at the moment—you'll hear everything soon.'

Replacing the instrument, Lisa felt a surge of envy. Olivia had got what she wanted and would probably experience more happiness than she, Lisa, would ever know. Slowly she sipped the mineral water, hoping it would revive her. Her work in the surgery this morning had, she knew, been dull and uninspired. Fortunately there had been no complicated cases, and thankfully there were no operations awaiting her. She told herself sternly that she must get a grip on herself or her work would deteriorate and her patients would suffer. She must face reality, accept it, and concentrate on the other love in her life—that of her profession. It was the only way out of the miserable tangle into which she had got trapped. Gradually she began to feel stronger and, getting up, she prepared to go back to the surgery. It was then that the telephone rang again. This time it was Barbara ringing on the extension.

'Lisa—Mrs Marsden rang from Valley Farm. Andrew has had an accident there. He says it's not serious, but he can't drive his car and she wants you to go over, see to his next patient—a cow with milk fever — and drive Andrew back. I've tried to get Roger in case you can't go, but he's out somewhere.'

Rushing down to the surgery, Lisa hurriedly filled her case from the dispensary, and Barbara gave more details as she handed over an obstetric gown.

'Andrew was ringing a bull and was caught off his guard. The bull jerked his head violently and Andrew was thrown to the ground, hitting his head on the concrete yard. He was dazed for a few moments, and although he maintains he's OK now Mrs Marsden says he must have suffered mild concussion and won't let him deal with the cow or drive himself back. Her husband is at the market and there's no one else available.'

Lisa's heart was racing as she got into her car. Andrew hurt — taken off his guard. That must be her fault. He had also probably slept badly and, like her, been tired and distracted in his work. Full of remorse, she arrived at the farm to find Mrs Marsden plying him with hot, sweet tea and consoling talk.

He looked up as she came into the kitchen, shrugged his shoulders, and said ruefully, 'It was my own damn fault. Sheer carelessness. Actually I'm perfectly all right now, but Mrs Marsden is a bit over-protective.' He looked reproachfully at the farmer's wife. 'Believe it or not, she's taken my car keys away.'

Mrs Marsden said firmly, 'Well, I wanted to get the doctor, but Mr Morland wouldn't hear of it and was all for carrying on. He says I'm making an unnecessary fuss, but I don't think I am, do you?'

'You did the right thing, Mrs Marsden,' Lisa said. 'Now, about that cow. Is there anyone with her?'

'Yes, the herdsman is waiting. He was helping Mr Morland with the bull. Mind you, we really should have had another man on the job as well. Pete offered to drive Mr Morland back, but that would have meant leaving the cow, so I thought it best to get you. By the way, don't worry about the bull. Luckily Mr Morland had just fixed it when the bull knocked him down.'

Well, thank goodness for that, Lisa muttered to herself as she went across the yard. Ringing a bull was not the kind of job she fancied. She still blamed herself for Andrew's accident. Remembering the way in which she had rebuffed him and how he had slammed out of her flat. . . She sighed. He was probably still angry, and that accounted for his distraction when dealing with the bull.

Pete, the herdsman, greeted her cheerfully, but, seeing that she looked worried, he said, 'Upset you, has it, miss? But it's not very serious. Mr Morland will be OK. He's tough. It's not the first time he's taken a tumble. And I've taken a few in my time.' He grinned. 'As a matter of fact, I was kicked by a cow the other day, and that was my own fault. I was worried about my wife, who had just gone into hospital to have our baby, and my mind wasn't on the job I was doing. When my wife heard about it she only laughed and said it was nothing to what she'd been through.' He paused and added reflectively, 'Got to concentrate all the time when you're dealing with animals.'

Lisa nodded. His light-hearted attitude only made her feel even more remorseful, and she felt certain now that she was reponsible for Andrew's accident. She drew a long breath and told herself that she must not let that guilty feeling distract her while dealing with the cow she had come to attend.

Pulling herself together, she looked around, and the herdsman said, 'There she is, miss, lying down over there and looking very miserable, poor thing.'

Although it was a comparatively simple job to do, it was always rather spectacular, the way in which the cow rose to her feet as soon as she had received the injection of a whole bottle of calcium borogluconate.

The herdsman said, 'You can leave her to me now, miss. I reckon she'll be OK now that the calcium level is back to normal.' He paused. 'In spite of all these new scientific methods, that's one of the treatments that doesn't change, does it?'

Back in the farmhouse she saw that Andrew looked much better and, as he stood up ready to leave, she said hesitatingly, 'Would you like to take my arm?'

He raised his eyebrows mockingly. 'You women! You'd think the bull had gored me. No need to make such a fuss.' There was a note of irritation in his voice, but, turning to Mrs Marsden, he said, 'All the same, I'm very grateful for the way you've lavished tea on me. It pulled me together in no time at all.'

Mrs Marsden was still concerned, however, and continued giving advice as she went out into the yard with them. Andrew looked ruefully at his car as they walked past it.

'Seems silly to leave it here when I'm quite capable of driving myself back. Still——' he shrugged '—since you've been good enough to come. . .' He paused as he settled himself in the passenger seat of Lisa's car. 'Perhaps if you can find the time tomorrow you wouldn't mind driving me over here to pick it up.'

Lisa nodded doubtfully, but resolved not to argue, though she was convinced that he ought to rest for one day at least. He stayed silent for most of the journey back, and when for a quick moment she glanced anxiously at him he snapped,

'For heaven's sake! Don't keep fussing. I'm perfectly OK. I'm just mad at myself for being such a damn fool.'

'I expect you were tired,' she suggested mildly, then quickly regretted what she had said, but he merely nodded,

'Yes. I'd had a bad night, but that's no excuse. One should never let one's personal feelings interfere with one's work.'

She pondered this for a few minutes, then impulsively she said, 'I feel responsible. That quarrel we had last night——'

'What quarrel?' His voice was cold. 'I was under the impression that we had settled everything. We now know exactly where we stand with regard to each other.'

She said no more. Her heart felt like lead, but, taking her cue from him, she managed to keep cool and distant. Pulling up outside his house, she said, 'You will go to bed and rest, won't you?'

'Of course. I'm not a fool. But for goodness' sake don't exaggerate things. I'll be OK in the morning.'

She looked closely at him as he began to get out of the car, saw that he was still pale, and said carefully, 'I or, if you'd rather, Roger can do your work tomorrow. Surely it would be better——'

He interrupted sharply, 'I told you not to exaggerate. I don't like being cosseted.' Reaching for his door key, she saw him sway a little, and was out of her car in a flash.

'Andrew—give me your key and hold on to me. Is your housekeeper indoors?'

He pulled himself together. 'No. She's got a week off. For heaven's sake. . .' He found his key and, putting it in the lock, opened the door and went into the hall, followed closely by Lisa. He turned. 'What are you doing?'

She looked up from searching on the telephone table. 'I'm looking for your doctor's number. You know very well you're concussed.'

'Only very slightly, and I know what to do. Now leave that that phone alone. I don't want my arrangements altered by a doctor. I've got a full week ahead. Besides, the day after tomorrow I've arranged to pick up Isabel, and that's priority number one.' He turned before going upstairs and gave her a grim little smile. 'Now stop following me. You'll be offering to undress me next.'

She flushed, but stayed watching until he reached the top. Then, as he went towards a bedroom door, he turned again and added, 'Mind what I say. No ringing the doctor.'

She went back to her car reluctantly, and just before getting in she caught sight of him at an upper window. He waved cheerfully and, half reassured, she drove slowly away. Probably she was being over-solicitous. Nevertheless she would tell Roger and then she would have no need to feel responsible for him. Then, suddenly, something like a sharp pain shot through her. Who on earth was Isabel? His priority number one, he had said. He had said her name softly, almost caressingly. It sounded like a death knell to her hopes, faint though she knew them to be, and only now did she really admit to them. How could she have ever imagined that one day Andrew might fall in love with her? Andrew had spoken as though Lisa knew all about Isabel, but how could she? She realised now that she knew nothing of his private life, and numb with shock, she looked into a dark future.

On arrival at the surgery she went quickly up to her flat, thankful that the nurses were temporarily absent. A cup of strong black coffee and perhaps then she would be able to face the inevitable questions about Andrew's accident without betraying the fact that her whole world seemed to have collapsed around her.

Half an hour later, revived and in full control of herself, she went down to the surgery and found with cold satisfaction that she was able to describe what had happened without giving away the fact that, although Andrew had been physically stunned, she herself had been knocked out emotionally. She had found an inner strength which enabled her to accept a situation that, she acknowledged bitterly, she ought to have foreseen. Andrew had found happiness and, in some strange way, it confirmed to her that she loved him even more deeply than she had realised. His happiness mattered more than any pain she herself felt, and that knowledge killed all self-pity. Her task now was to keep her love hidden from him and the rest of the world. Above all, she told herself, she must show no animosity or jealousy towards Isabel when they met.

Later in the day Roger rang with the news that Andrew was back to his usual self.

'He's had a good rest, and when the doctor arrived. . .' He laughed. 'Oh, yes, as soon as you told me I rang the doctor and asked him to come, in spite of Andrew's protests. He said it was nothing serious, told him to take tomorrow off—I'll do his calls—then he could work as usual.'

Lisa said, 'Well, he won't be working the day after tomorrow. He told me he was going to fetch. . .'

She hesitated, and Roger put in quickly, 'Oh, yes— Isabel. For the moment I'd forgotten.' He laughed again. 'She'll complete his recovery. He's been talking about her all day. Anyway, we've got to get his car back, so I suggest that tomorrow after morning surgery you drive me over to the Marsdens' farm. I'll pick it up and do any farm calls that have come in. Is that OK?'

Evening surgery, much to Lisa's relief, was quiet, and when it was over she went up to her flat, hoping that there would be no emergencies. She needed time to strengthen her newly found calm and to take a steady look at what the future held for her. An hour's reflection showed her the way. She must enlarge her horizons with regard to both work and recreation. Professionally, it would be easy. She would keep up to date with all the latest scientific developments, attend veterinary meetings and conferences, and absorb herself in the career she had chosen. That would also provide her with other outlets, for there were friends of college days with whom she had lost touch, and friendships could be renewed. It was no use bewailing her fate. She must be thankful that she had work to do that she loved and into which she could put all her energy.

Next morning she went into the surgery strengthened by her resolutions. As the waiting-room filled up she was kept so busy that her personal troubles faded into the background. Problems seemed to be the order of the day — problems sometimes caused by the owners themselves, such as a Persian cat whose coat had been so neglected that it was impossible to comb out without putting the unfortunate animal under a general anaesthetic, dogs with neglected skin troubles and others with digestive upsets caused by injudicious feeding. Then a middle-aged couple brought in a puppy with one eye half closed, and the bluish-coloured interior could hardly be seen.

'The last of the litter,' said the man. 'We thought it would gradually get better, but —— ' he shook his head sadly ' — it's got to be put to sleep, I'm afraid.'

With difficulty Lisa was able to convince them that this condition was one that could be put right by an operation. 'It's called an entropion,' she said. 'The lower lid is turned in and the eyelashes are in direct contact with the eye. So it's a question of plastic surgery. I shall take a piece of skin — the shape of a half-moon — from below the eyelid, draw the skin together, pull the eyelid down, and stitch on the piece. In about ten days I'll take the stitches out and the eye will be normal. Now——' Lisa looked at the worried couple questioningly '—shall I do this operation or would you rather I put the puppy to sleep?'

The owners glanced at each other and the man said, 'Well, as you can see, this pup is a thoroughbred and quite valuable, so we'll have it done. Mind you, it had better be a success—I'm not paying for a botched-up job.'

The operation was fixed for the following day, and when the couple had gone Barbara said grimly, 'What an unpleasant man. I'll bet he wouldn't speak to his doctor like that.'

Sally looked at Lisa curiously. 'Doesn't that kind of threatening attitude make you nervous while you're doing such a delicate operation?'

Lisa shook her head. 'No. I just don't think about it. I'm only concerned for the dog. The patient must always come first.'

But her last case was a very different one. A young Pit Bull terrier came in, held on a strong chain by a young man with a grim face. 'Got to be put down, miss,' he said angrily. 'A fine little dog, too, but he's attacked two children and one of them is in hospital. There's no option.'

It was all over in a very short time, but by then Sally's tears were flowing. Barbara hastily produced coffee, and as they sat down Sally managed a watery smile.

'Sometimes I think I'll never get used to this kind of thing, but I really am trying. Roger says I've got to be realistic, and I know he's right.'

Barbara said sardonically, 'Roger's words seem to carry more weight with you than ours do. We've been trying to tell you that for ages.'

Sally brightened. 'I think he's wonderful—so understanding.' Then suddenly, with a quick glance at Lisa, she said, 'All the same, I'm a bit worried by something he said yesterday. Apparently Andrew is going to fetch someone called Isabel tomorrow. I gather she's going to stay with them, because he said they were getting things ready for her, and he was beginning to tell me more when the telephone rang and he had to rush off. But not before he muttered something about Andrew having described her as absolutely beautiful.' She frowned. 'I know it's Andrew's affair, but I just hope that Roger won't fall for her as well.'

'You're over-reacting,' Barbara said scornfully, 'letting your imagination run away with you as usual.' She paused, then added thoughtfully. 'It's strange, though, isn't it? I wonder who she is.' She turned to Lisa. 'Do you know anything about her?'

Lisa took a firm grip on herself. 'Haven't a clue,' she said lightly, and glanced at her watch. 'I must fly. Roger will be waiting for me to go and fetch Andrew's car.'

CHAPTER TEN

LISA's hopes of getting Roger to talk about Isabel were quickly dashed. In answer to her enquiry about Andrew he told her that he was fully recovered, then, just as she was composing a tactful question, he began to talk about Sally.

At last, he said, he had met the girl he wanted to marry. There was no doubt about it — he was seriously in love. He proceeded to enlarge on the subject to such an extent that Lisa gradually gave up all hope of changing the conversation. Resignedly she reassured him when he asked her anxiously if she thought Sally reciprocated his feelings; at least, she added cautiously, that was the impression she had gathered from the way Sally spoke about him. Then, of course, she had to repeat in detail any remarks that could encourage him to be optimistic, and by the time they arrived at the Marsdens' farm she knew that her opportunity had passed.

After giving details of Andrew's recovery to Mrs Marsden, she refused coffee on the grounds that she was pressed for time. Then she drove back to the surgery, where she found all preparations had been made for the entropion operation. She worked in silence, absorbed in the delicate cutting and stitching, and, with Barbara presiding over the anaesthetic machine and Sally handing her the necessary instruments, the operation was completed to her entire satisfaction. Standing back from the table, she surveyed her work with a sigh of relief.

'In ten days' time when the stitches are taken out the

eye — apart from a little bruising, which will soon wear off — will be completely normal,' she said and, turning, she smiled at the two nurses. 'Thank you both for your help.'

Sally, who had been unusually calm, said thoughtfully, 'It was marvellous. Really interesting. What's more, for the first time, I felt so involved that I never had any qualms.' She paused. 'Could Roger do that?'

Lisa laughed. 'Of course he could. Just the same as he could do far more difficult operations than this one. You mustn't think I'm any cleverer than any other vet. We're all trained the same way. Of course, some specialise in the work they prefer, but we can all turn our hands to anything that comes along. It's a very wide field and a very rewarding one. I personally wouldn't want to be in any other profession.'

Sally nodded solemnly. 'I begin to see what you mean. Roger said something like that the other evening. He also said that any girl considering marriage to a vet ought to think very carefully before she committed herself.' She hesitated. 'Why do you think he said that to me?'

Lisa and Barbara exchanged quizzical looks, and Barbara laughed. 'Don't tell us you haven't the least idea. You must know that he's sounding you out — testing the water before plunging in, so to speak.'

The glow of pleasure on Sally's face told its own story, and Lisa felt a sudden pang of envy. She sighed, then, pulling herself together, she said, 'Well, I know it's late for coffee, but let's have some just the same.'

They were discussing Andrew's accident and Lisa was just hoping to bring up the subject of Isabel when there was a tap at the door and Olivia walked into the room.

'Do you mind if I join you?' she asked. 'I've got some news that I think will interest you all. Also I want you to come to an informal party ——'

She broke off as Sally, glancing out of the window, said, 'Here's Andrew — he'll think we do nothing but drink coffee.'

Olivia looked pleased. 'I'm glad he's come. My news will surprise him — that's if he doesn't know already.'

Lisa looked at her curiously, but she stayed silent until Andrew entered. Sally had judged rightly, for he frowned a little as he gazed at them.

'What's this? A coffee-morning?'

The implied criticism was unwelcome to Lisa. Surely she, as a partner, could do what she liked in her surgery? She was about to point this out briskly, but Barbara forestalled her by telling him about the entropion operation, and the slight tension lifted as he sat down beside Olivia.

'Well, I might as well join you. I'm waiting for Roger to come back with my car.' He turned to Olivia. 'Anything wrong with Spot?'

She shook her head. 'No, he's fine. I've just come in to ask you all to come to a small informal party.'

'All of us?' Andrew looked doubtful. 'That might be a little difficult. Is it the house-warming party you mentioned?'

'No. I've let that slide. This is something much more important. David and I. . .' She paused and surveyed the company with a jubilant air. 'David and I have just got engaged and we'd like to thank you all for bringing us together.'

The dramatic announcement produced the appropriate effect, and when the exclamations and congratulations had died down Andrew rose to his feet.

'This calls for something more potent than mere coffee,' he said smilingly. 'I'll just go and fetch a bottle — I'll only be a few minutes.'

'No need,' said Olivia calmly. 'See. . .' She opened a capacious bag standing on the floor beside her. 'Champagne and glasses. Will you open the bottle, please, Andrew?'

As they toasted her and the absent David, Lisa watched her a little wistfully. It was plain to see that Olivia was very happy. She had gone all out to find an attractive man who could give her what she wanted and, having succeeded, she was now in a glow of contentment. She would probably, Lisa thought, have been just as happy if she had been announcing her engagement to Andrew or even Roger. Sipping thoughtfully at her champagne, she wondered suddenly if she was becoming hard and cynical. Glancing up, she caught Andrew's gaze fixed on her, and as their eyes met his mouth twisted in amusement.

'Romance seems to be in the air,' he said lightly and turned to Sally. 'From what I gather from Roger. . . well, let's put it like this — will you be the next?'

There was laughter as Sally choked over her glass, then Olivia said purposefully, 'This party — we're having it in David's house tomorrow evening. Please do come — all of you. Surely it can be managed?'

Andrew looked thoughtful, then with a questioning glance at Lisa he said, 'Why not? If anything urgent should come in I'm sure you'll understand if one or other of us has to leave suddenly.' He paused. 'I myself may be a little late in arriving, but I'll turn up eventually.'

Olivia got up. 'I have to go. By the way, if any of you wants to bring a friend along that will be OK.'

'There you are.' Sally turned to Barbara. 'You can bring your George.' She giggled. 'We'll all be in pairs. I'll be with Roger, you and George and——' she hesitated '— that leaves Andrew and Lisa. Even if they're not speaking to each other they can always talk to Isabel. That is, of course if he brings her along so that we can all meet her.'

Carefully avoiding looking at Andrew, and thankful that Olivia was engrossed in packing away the glasses, Lisa said coolly, 'It's a good job there's no more champagne. It's obviously gone to Sally's head.'

She went to the door with Olivia, then, as the nurses went off to the recovery-room, she came back to find herself alone with Andrew. Now, she thought, this is the moment to find out more about Isabel, but she hesitated, unable to find the right words, and all she said was, 'I'm glad to see that you're fully recovered from your accident.'

'It was all rather exaggerated——' he shrugged '—but I'm grateful for your help.' He strolled over to the window. 'Ah, here comes Roger with my car.' He turned. 'Well, I'll see you tomorrow evening. It's my day off tomorrow.'

Here was her chance, and she took it quickly. 'Will you bring your friend Isabel to Olivia's party?'

For a moment his eyes flickered and his mouth twisted at the corner, then he said drily, 'I think it might be a little overwhelming for her—all those strangers at once. Anyway, you'll meet her soon enough. All I hope is that you'll be friends.'

She said no more, but his words echoed in her mind long after he had gone. 'You'll meet her soon enough'. . . The phrase seemed ominous. It implied so much. Evidently his relationship with Isabel was going to cause talk, but he expected that Lisa would make a friend of the mysterious girl who was going to live in his house. Of course it might be only a temporary stay, but his last words had made it sound more than that.

It was the last straw, she told herself desolately. Trying hard to accept the unhappy situation, she acknowledged that she ought to have expected something like this to happen. After all, she knew very little about Andrew and nothing at all about his emotional life apart from the unhappy episode with Jane. The trouble was that she had read too much into the fact that he had kissed her, had said things that seemed to indicate he was beginning to care for her, when in reality it meant absolutely nothing. If Isabel meant so much to Andrew, then surely the inevitable would follow? Their engagement — marriage. The partner's wife with whom it would be necessary to come into close contact. The thought of Andrew and Isabel as man and wife — that was the worst thing of all to imagine.

A quotation rose in her mind and she said the words aloud. '"'Tis better to have loved and lost than never to have loved at all".' Oh, no, she thought bitterly, it was far better never to have loved at all. The only glimmer of light at the end of the long, dark tunnel stretching ahead of her was the thought that if it all got too much then she would make her escape, resign her partnership, and begin a new life as far away as possible from the man she loved so hopelessly. It would have to be much later — she couldn't possibly change her mind again so soon without looking utterly ridiculous.

The next day, with the prospect of Olivia's party that evening looming ahead, Lisa managed nevertheless to keep her mind on her work, giving loving care to her patients and coping cheerfully with their owners. Sally was in effervescent mood and only once did she mention Isabel again. Hanging up her surgery overall after evening surgery, she said, 'I've tried to sound Roger out about his possible reaction to the beautiful Isabel and I don't think I've anything to fear. He said —— ' she laughed self-consciously ' — small and cuddly was more his preference, from which I gather that Isabel must be tall and — well, not cuddly.' She giggled. 'This tall, beautiful creature — I can't wait to meet her, can you?'

Lisa took the news calmly and merely smiled, but the

extra blow added further pain which she did her best to endure bravely.

On arrival at the party she found it was already in full swing and after a quick, searching look she was relieved to see that Andrew was not yet there. Soon she was moving from group to group, joining in the laughter and congratulations and putting on a good show of thoroughly enjoying herself. Introduced by Olivia to her doctor brother, she kept up an animated conversation and kept her back resolutely to the door when, at last, with a sudden leap of her heart she heard Andrew's voice. But her hand trembled a little and the doctor said jovially, 'Good job your glass is empty. I'll get it refilled for you.'

Standing alone for a few moments, she was about to join another group when she felt a hand on her shoulder.

'Lisa. . .' The deep voice made her turn to face him, and with a little gasp of surprise she saw that he was on his own.

'All right,' he said sharply. 'No need to make it so apparent that you don't like me to touch you.' He took his hand away. 'All I want to say is that you look wonderful in that blue dress.' He paused. 'Why do you always stiffen when I make a personal remark? Am I the only man in the world who isn't allowed to pay you a compliment? That doctor brother of Olivia's was looking at you very appreciatively, I noticed. Is he managing to draw you out of your shell?'

With an effort Lisa laughed his question off, then she asked casually, 'Isabel — you didn't bring her?'

A muscle throbbed in his temple and he smiled crookedly. For a moment a wild hope rose in Lisa's mind. Perhaps she had let him down — even found someone else — but she quickly dismissed that thought as unworthy. After all, she wanted him to be happy.

'This kind of thing isn't her scene,' he said drily, 'but come back with me when this——' he indicated the crowded room ' — is over. I'd like you to meet her.' He turned. 'Here comes your medical admirer. Don't let him offer to take you home. I'll be waiting for you.'

There was something strange in his manner, but as the party gathered momentum she had no opportunity to give him any more thought. Only when the atmosphere grew altogether too hot and smoky was she able to consider leaving. When she went up to thank her host and hostess and say goodbye, Olivia said smilingly, 'I believe Andrew is waiting outside for you. He asked me to remind you.'

Lisa frowned to herself as she went outside. It was late and she was tired, and that would be her excuse. She certainly didn't want to meet Isabel, and most probably Isabel would not want to meet her.

Andrew was standing beside his car, and as she approached he opened the passenger door. She shook her head firmly. 'No, Andrew. I'm looking forward to meeting Isabel, but not tonight. I'm too tired. I've had a busy day.'

He gazed at her steadily as they stood in the illuminated driveway. 'You don't look tired to me. You look as fresh as when I spoke to you a couple of hours ago. Besides, I want to have a serious talk with you about something that can't wait until tomorrow.'

She looked puzzled. 'If it's something urgent, then you can tell me now. Is it an emergency?'

He shook his head, and even in the artificial light she could see that his face looked strained and anxious. He said, 'No veterinary emergency. A human one that must be discussed.' He shut the door he was holding. 'I've just realised you've got your own car here, so I'll follow you to your flat, then you can transfer to my car.'

Bewildered, she said no more, but, still determined not to give in, she drove quickly back and put her car into the garage. She was walking round to the outside entrance to her flat when suddenly he came up and took her arm.

'I won't keep you long, but you must come. There's something between us that must be sorted out.'

Reluctantly she capitulated, disturbed and apprehensive at what lay ahead. He drove in silence and she could sense that he, also, was in a highly nervous state. Meeting Isabel was obviously an excuse that he was using in order to tell her of something very important — probably, in spite of his denial, something to do with the practice. Either he was going to leave or she was going to be asked to resign after all. Her mind was racing as he pulled into the driveway of his house, and she watched in troubled silence as he put his key in the door. He turned to let her precede him into the large hallway, then as she waited to be shown which way to go he stood still and looked at her searchingly. Embarrassed, she asked nervously, 'What's wrong? Why are you looking at me like that?'

'I was just wondering,' he said quietly, 'wondering about something I've been told concerning you.'

Curiosity aroused to an almost feverish degree, she asked tremulously, 'What is it? Good or bad?'

He hesitated. 'I'll tell you soon. I just hope it's right, that's all. Meantime, come and meet Isabel.'

Lisa's heart sank. Why, oh why had she allowed him to bring her here? Late as it was, tired after the party and the champagne she had been obliged to drink, she was in no state to control her emotions. She drew a long, deep breath, telling herself that she must on no account show her real feelings of bitter envy towards the new love in Andrew's life. He went to open a door, pausing for a moment to say, 'She has been staying with my brother and his wife, but now that I've settled in here she's come to live with me.'

As the impact of his words hit her, Lisa swallowed hard. Was he being purposefully cruel? Had he guessed that she was in love with him and was about to force her to face up to the hopelessness of her situation? Was he. . .? Suddenly she gasped as he opened the door and a magnificent red setter dog rushed forward.

'Meet Isabel. . .' Andrew caressed the beautiful creature whose feathery tail was waving wildly at the sight of her master. 'Isn't she lovely?'

Stunned and shocked, Lisa felt tears well up in her eyes and run unheeded down her cheeks. Unable to hide her joy, she stammered, 'I thought — I thought — oh, Andrew, why didn't you tell me?'

His hand pressed down on Isabel's glossy head, quelling her exuberance, then, turning to Lisa, he gazed at her with an unreadable expression in his eyes. He seemed to have difficulty with his breathing, but at last he asked softly, 'Why are you crying?'

She shook her head hopelessly, took the handkerchief he held out to her, and wiped her eyes.

'I can't explain. I simply can't.' She paused. 'It was a shock. I was expecting. . .' She stopped and he nodded slowly.

'You were expecting to meet a beautiful girl — isn't that it?' Suddenly he swallowed hard and his voice trembled. 'And if your reaction means what I was told, then. . .'

He stopped and they stood facing each other in a silence that was fraught with meaning. But to Lisa the meaning was far from clear. Puzzling over his last words, she asked, 'What on earth do you mean? Who and what are you talking about?'

'I'm talking about your reaction to Isabel. To the fact

that you expected I had a beautiful girlfriend. They said——'

'They?' Lisa's voice, even in her own ears, sounded cold as ice—cold as the chill that was gathering round her heart.

'Sally, Barbara, Roger—who else could it be?' His tone was steady now. 'It was a kind of test.'

Suddenly her frigidity turned to blazing anger. 'So it was a put-up job between you! For some reason the four of you decided to fool me into thinking. . .' She paused for a moment, then flared out, 'Why? What was the point of it? Was it just to make me a laughing-stock? What a childish thing to do. I suppose it was Sally's idea.'

He said evenly, 'Yes, it was Sally's idea. She said it would prove something of which she was absolutely certain—something that I personally refused to believe.' His eyes searched her face as though he was trying to read her mind, then he said, 'Don't look at me like that, Lisa. Just listen to me and try to understand. Sally told Roger that she was convinced that you were beginning to care for me—no, wait! Don't fly off the handle till I've had my say. . .' He swallowed hard then went on slowly, 'She—Sally—said it might be a good idea to test your reactions when you eventually found out that my imaginary girlfriend—an idea they thought out when I first mentioned Isabel—was only a dog.' He shook his head. 'I ought not to have gone along with them, but——' he paused '—well, I was getting desperate. Sally said——'

He stopped abruptly as Lisa, her eyes blazing, said violently, 'Of all the cruel things to do!' She lifted her hand, but he caught her wrist and held it tightly.

'Lisa! I said wait until you've heard me out. I only agreed because——'

She interrupted fiercely, twisting her wrist in his

grasp. 'I don't want to hear any more. You've humiliated me enough.' She choked on a sob. 'Let me go,
please. You're hurting me.'

Suddenly, distracting them both, Isabel began to bark
in alarm as she sensed the tense atmosphere, and
Andrew released his hold and bent down to soothe the
troubled animal. Then, looking up, he saw Lisa wincing
as she rubbed her wrist. Instantly he was contrite.

'Lisa, darling, I'm sorry. I didn't mean to hurt you. I
love you so much — I didn't realise what I was doing.'

She stared at him in astonishment, her brilliant eyes
still wet with tears, and, taking advantage of her
amazed silence, he rushed on, 'Yes, I love you, Lisa,
love you to distraction. It was burning me up, and
Roger couldn't fail to see it. He told Sally and she, in
turn, said that although you did your best to try and
prove the opposite she wasn't fooled. So then she
suggested that the way for me to find out was to make
you — well — a bit jealous. Barbara agreed, and between
them all they hatched up a plot around the arrival of
Isabel.' He drew a long breath, then as she still said
nothing he said bitterly, 'But they were wrong, weren't
they? And I've made a ghastly mistake.'

Still gazing at him incredulously, Lisa simply could
not take in what she heard. Her rage was simmering;
she could only feel violent resentment as she remembered the veiled hints that had made her jump to the
conclusion the others had meant her to reach, and now
all she wanted was to save her face. At last, looking at
him with all the scorn she could muster, she said, 'Don't
try any more tricks on me, please. I'll never, never
believe another word you say.'

Turning quickly she went out of the house and
walked swiftly along the quiet road until she reached
her flat. Once inside, she began to make her preparations for bed, still in a state of cold fury. Then,

suddenly, with startling clarity, Andrew's words echoed in her mind. 'I love you, Lisa, love you to distraction.' She stood rigid, the memory of his white, drawn face stabbing her heart, and the bitterness in his voice when he said that he had made a ghastly mistake made her echo those same words aloud. Was it true? Had he really said that? But yes. He was desperate, he had said; it was burning him up. . . Oh, God! What had she done? Refused to believe him, thrown his love back in his face in her anxiety to save her own. . . She stared ahead unseeingly for a few minutes, then suddenly she began to weep. It was some time before she gained control of herself, then she glanced at her watch. Nearly midnight, but she would never sleep until she had spoken to Andrew. Still sobbing quietly, she picked up the telephone. At the sound of his voice her tears flowed again and all she could say was, 'Andrew — please come over here. Please — it's urgent.'

She heard him say, 'Lisa — what's the matter? Have you had an accident?' but, unable to find any words, she replaced the receiver and sat numbed and frightened at what she had done so impulsively. She heard his car race into the yard, heard him running up the stairs, and, getting up slowly, she went to the door. His face was even paler than when she had left him, but as he saw her tear-stained cheeks he held out his arms and she went into them blindly.

'Lisa — my darling, darling Lisa — will you ever forgive me? I've hurt you so much — I've made you ill. What can I do to put things right?'

Lisa drew back in his arms and gazed up at him steadily. 'You can answer a question,' she said.

'A question? Is that all?' He stared down at her, a puzzled, worried look in his eyes. 'How can that put things right?'

She hesitated, then, drawing a long nervous breath,

she said, 'Why did you say you. . .?' She gulped and began again. 'Why did you. . .? Oh, Andrew, do you really love me?'

For a moment he seemed too stunned to answer. Then, almost grimly, he said, 'I love you with all my heart, Lisa. It's the real thing — the kind of love that lasts a lifetime. There'll never be anyone else for me.' He stopped for a moment and she saw deep sadness in his eyes. 'Now I must ask you this. Are you trying to hurt me the way I hurt you? I know you don't love me — the others got it all wrong.'

Lisa's voice shook. 'No, they didn't. They were right.' She saw him gasp, and her voice trembled even more as she said, 'I do love you, Andrew, darling. I really do. With the same kind of love —'

She got no further, for he was holding her so fiercely that she could hardly breathe. His lips hovered over hers, then, unexpectedly, he drew back, lifted her face so that he could look deeply into her eyes and said, 'You're sure? You're absolutely sure? You won't change your mind again? You will marry me? I couldn't bear. . .' His voice broke and he buried his face in her hair.

So many questions, all born of agonies of uncertainty. . . Lisa was stricken with remorse. She had vacillated so much — handing in her resignation, retracting it, threatening once more to leave. . . She had been as changeable as the weather. She had been in a continual state of confusion — no wonder there had been so many misunderstandings between them.

Reaching up, she put her arm round his neck and pulled his head down. Against his searching lips she said softly, 'I'll never, never change again. This is forever.'

He kissed her then, one long, passionate kiss in which their two beings seemed to merge into one. Then as they drew apart for a moment he said, 'Tomorrow we'll celebrate, my darling. Out to dinner, then back to my house with lovely Isabel and glorious music. Music that says it all.' He paused, smiling down at her in a way that melted her heart. 'Beethoven — the "Appassionata" Sonata. Do you think that would be appropriate?'

Lisa studied his face carefully, saw the flame of desire at the back of his eyes, and said softly, 'Just the right accompaniment to love.'

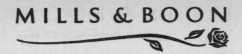

MILLS & BOON

HEARTS OF FIRE by Miranda Lee

Welcome to our compelling family saga set in the glamorous world of opal dealing in Australia. Laden with dark secrets, forbidden desires and scandalous discoveries, **Hearts of Fire** unfolds over a series of 6 books, but each book also features a passionate romance with a happy ending and can be read independently.

Book 1: SEDUCTION & SACRIFICE
Published: April 1994   *FREE* with Book 2

Lenore had loved Zachary Marsden secretly for years. Loyal, handsome and protective, Zachary was the perfect husband. Only Zachary would never leave his wife…would he?

Book 2: DESIRE & DECEPTION
Published: April 1994   Price £2.50

Jade had a name for Kyle Armstrong: *Mr Cool*. He was the new marketing manager at Whitmore Opals—the job *she* coveted. However, the more she tried to hate this usurper, the more she found him attractive…

Book 3: PASSION & THE PAST
Published: May 1994   Price £2.50

Melanie was intensely attracted to Royce Grantham—which shocked her! She'd been so sure after the tragic end of her marriage that she would never feel for any man again. How strong was her resolve not to repeat past mistakes?

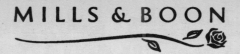

MILLS & BOON

HEARTS OF FIRE by Miranda Lee

Book 4: FANTASIES & THE FUTURE
Published: June 1994   Price £2.50

The man who came to mow the lawns was more stunning than any of Ava's fantasies, though she realised that Vincent Morelli thought she was just another rich, lonely housewife looking for excitement! But, Ava knew that her narrow, boring existence was gone forever...

Book 5: SCANDALS & SECRETS
Published: July 1994   Price £2.50

Celeste Campbell had lived on her hatred of Byron Whitmore for twenty years. Revenge was sweet...until news reached her that Byron was considering remarriage. Suddenly she found she could no longer deny all those long-buried feelings for him...

Book 6: MARRIAGE & MIRACLES
Published: August 1994   Price £2.50

Gemma's relationship with Nathan was in tatters, but her love for him remained intact—she was going to win him back! Gemma knew that Nathan's terrible past had turned his heart to stone, and she was asking for a miracle. But it was possible that one could happen, wasn't it?

Don't miss all six books!

LOVE ON CALL
4 FREE BOOKS AND 2 FREE GIFTS
FROM MILLS & BOON

Capture all the drama and emotion of a hectic medical world when you accept 4 Love on Call romances PLUS a cuddly teddy bear and a mystery gift - absolutely FREE and without obligation. And, if you choose, go on to enjoy 4 exciting Love on Call romances every month for only £1.80 each! Be sure to return the coupon below today to: Mills & Boon Reader Service, FREEPOST, PO Box 236, Croydon, Surrey CR9 9EL.

--- **NO STAMP REQUIRED** ---

YES! Please rush me 4 FREE Love on Call books and 2 FREE gifts! Please also reserve me a Reader Service subscription, which means I can look forward to receiving 4 brand new Love on Call books for only £7.20 every month, postage and packing FREE. If I choose not to subscribe, I shall write to you within 10 days and still keep my FREE books and gifts. I may cancel or suspend my subscription at any time. I am over 18 years. Please write in BLOCK CAPITALS.

Ms/Mrs/Miss/Mr _____ **EP63D**

Address _____

_____

Postcode _____ Signature _____

mps
MAILING
PREFERENCE
SERVICE

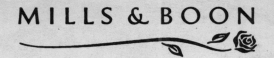

MILLS & BOON

LOVE ON CALL

The books for enjoyment this month are:

VET IN A QUANDARY Mary Bowring
NO SHADOW OF DOUBT Abigail Gordon
PRIORITY CARE Mary Hawkins
TO LOVE AGAIN Laura MacDonald

♥   ♥   ♥   ♥   ♥

Treats in store!

Watch next month for the following absorbing stories:

A MAN OF HONOUR Caroline Anderson
RUNNING AWAY Lilian Darcy
THE FRAGILE HEART Jean Evans
THE SENIOR PARTNER'S DAUGHTER Elizabeth Harrison

HEARTS OF FIRE

By Miranda Lee

HEARTS OF FIRE by Miranda Lee is a totally compelling six-part saga set in Australia's glamorous but cut-throat world of gem dealing.

Discover the passion, scandal, sin and finally the hope that exists between two fabulously rich families. You'll be hooked from the very first page…

Each of the six novels in this series features a gripping romance. And the first title **SEDUCTION AND SACRIFICE** can be yours absolutely FREE! You can also reserve the remaining five novels in this exciting series from Reader Service, delivered to your door for £2.50 each. And remember postage and packing is FREE!

MILLS & BOON READER SERVICE, FREEPOST, P.O. BOX 236, CROYDON CR9 9EL. TEL: 081-684 2141

- -

YES! Please send me my FREE book (part 1 in the Hearts of Fire series) and reserve me a subscription for the remaining 5 books in the series. I understand that you will send me one book each month and invoice me £2.50 each month.

NO STAMP NEEDED

MILLS & BOON READER SERVICE, FREEPOST, P.O. BOX 236, CROYDON CR9 9EL. TEL: 081-684 2141

Ms/Mrs/Miss/Mr: _____   EPHOF

Address _____

_____

_____

_____ Postcode _____